Candleshine

A Sequel to A Torch for Trinity

Colleen L. Reece

Thorndike Press • Waterville, Maine

Published in 2006 by arrangement with Colleen L. Reece.

Thorndike Press® Large Print Candlelight.

The tree indicium is a trademark of Thorndike Press.

The text of this Large Print edition is unabridged.
Other aspects of the book may vary from the original edition.

Set in 16 pt. Plantin by Christina S. Huff.

Printed in the United States on permanent paper.

Library of Congress Cataloging-in-Publication Data

Reece, Colleen L.
    Candleshine / by Colleen L. Reece.
        p. cm. — (Thorndike Press large print Candlelight)
    Sequel to: A torch for Trinity.
    ISBN 0-7862-8354-8 (lg. print : hc : alk. paper)
    1. World War, 1939–1945 — Fiction.   2. Nurses — Fiction.   3. Large type books.   I. Title.   II. Thorndike Press large print Candlelight series.
    PS3568.E3646C36 2006
    813'.54—dc22   2005031399

For good friends Al and Anna Smith, whose knowledge and experience of World War II enriched this book.

Special thanks go to Ron Wanttaja for his technical advice on airplanes.

As the Founder/CEO of NAVH, the only national health agency solely devoted to those who, although not totally blind, have an eye disease which could lead to serious visual impairment, I am pleased to recognize Thorndike Press* as one of the leading publishers in the large print field.

Founded in 1954 in San Francisco to prepare large print textbooks for partially seeing children, NAVH became the pioneer and standard setting agency in the preparation of large type.

Today, those publishers who meet our standards carry the prestigious "Seal of Approval" indicating high quality large print. We are delighted that Thorndike Press is one of the publishers whose titles meet these standards. We are also pleased to recognize the significant contribution Thorndike Press is making in this important and growing field.

Lorraine H. Marchi, L.H.D.
Founder/CEO
NAVH

* Thorndike Press encompasses the following imprints: Thorndike, Wheeler, Walker and Large Print Press.

One

Twin rows of stiffly starched, white-uniformed young women wearing white caps with the cherished black band — the result of three long years of hard work — lined the long hall. Of the original fifty who had enrolled in January 1939 at the Mercy Hospital School of Nursing in Seattle, Washington, thirty-six would complete the course. Behind the soon-to-be graduates stood gray-clad, white-bibbed underclassmen, their aprons, collars, cuffs, and unadorned caps spotless. Beginning probationers in blue breathlessly admired the thirty-six and dreamed of the day they would replace the senior nurses.

Three years . . . a moment, a lifetime. Candace Thatcher, nicknamed Candle-shine by family and friends, glanced at the nurse beside her. A wave of emotion rushed through her. What did the war-torn future hold for Connie Imoto, her best friend from the first day they entered training? Would the sadness that had lived in Connie's expressive eyes ever since the Japanese attack on Pearl Harbor — aptly described as "a date that will live in infamy" by President Franklin Delano Roosevelt — ever disappear?

For one cowardly moment she wished she had never left Cedar Ridge, Washington, her home. The peaceful mountain hamlet seemed far removed from war. Why should Tojo, Hitler, and Mussolini add to the pain and suffering nurses worked so hard to overcome?

She drew her slim body to its five-foot six-inch height, exactly six inches taller than Connie. If ever the rigid discipline and training of the past years must be practiced, that time was now. Her short, fair hair that turned up at the ends had been secured neatly under her cap; her blue eyes, normally lively with fun, had darkened with uncertainty. Only slightly out of line were the few tiny freckles that made her pink and white skin look like wild strawberries. In short, it was a face scrubbed and pleasant but not beautiful.

A slight ripple of movement heralded the slow procession into the large auditorium. Connie smiled tremulously and faced front as did Candleshine. Yet even this final walk seemed to fade when Candleshine confronted a multitude of searing, significant memories. . . .

"Hold him still!" yelled Bruce Thatcher to his pigtailed cousin.

"How do you hold a squirming cat still?" shot back Candleshine as she tightened her hold on the big yellow cat, protecting herself from his claws with layers of her cotton skirt.

Bruce carefully swabbed the long cut on the cat's back. "Now, whatever you do, don't let him go. This salve may sting but it will make him well."

Five minutes later the indignant but well-doctored tom escaped to the barn loft, muttering under his breath. Candleshine grinned. "By the time *you* get to medical school you'll be teaching *your* instructors."

Bruce's brown hair stood on end and his blue eyes laughed. "Don't forget you're going to be a nurse."

"I won't." She leaned back on the grass and stared up through the dappled shade of a big maple. "Bruce, I wish we were the same age and could go away together."

His laughter died. "I do, too, but since I'm more than five years older than you, we can't. I can just see you entering a school of nursing when you're thirteen!"

She smirked and her flaxen pigtails spilled to both sides of her head. "When I *do* get there, they'll say, 'Why, Miss Thatcher. You already know so much about the medical field we're going to give you your diploma. The world is just waiting for you and there's really no reason for you to spend three years repeating what you already know.' "

"So what *do* you know that so highly qualifies you, smarty?"

She sat up and ticked off on her fingers. "I know the name and location of every bone in the body. I —"

"You don't!"

"Do too. Think I could hear you say them over and over and not remember?" A little puff of exasperation colored her expressive face.

"Say them." The cousin who had adored Candleshine since she was born couldn't help teasing.

Candleshine adjusted imaginary glasses, took on the pompous air of a lecturer, and began. "Ladies and gentlemen, there are two hundred bones, exclusive of teeth, in the human body." In rapid-fire order she named them, accurately identifying their locations until Bruce interrupted her monotonic recital.

"Stop, stop, I'm convinced."

"Let that be a lesson to you," his companion admonished. She abandoned her pose and became pensive. "I wonder if I can stand to leave all this, even to be a nurse?"

Bruce's gaze followed her gesture. From the slight rise above the Thatcher home, once a one-room schoolhouse where Candleshine's mother Trinity taught all eight grades at a time, tall firs, rounded hills, and sharply rearing mountains basked in the late afternoon sunlight.

Bruce caught her mood. Not often did the reserved young man open his heart, even to his cousin and best friend. "I think knowing it — and your folks and mine — will always be here to come back to makes it easier for me to go and learn. Remember how your mother always quotes her grandmother about each person carrying a torch for God? And passing it on to the next generation? Besides, she even named you Candace because it means glittering, flowing white."

"I know." The girl's sunny nature didn't allow time for prolonged sadness. "White for a nurse's uniform. White for a bride."

"*Bride!* Better concentrate on being a

nurse first." Bruce sighed and stood, brushing off his old pants and shirt. "I have to get home and finish the chores." As he strode away with long steps he called over his shoulder, "Thanks for helping with the cat."

"Any time." Her contentment pealed out in a final, mocking laugh. Yet when the tall figure got smaller and smaller then vanished behind into the grove of trees that separated Will Thatcher's and Jamie Thatcher's land, she frowned. Some of the goldenness of the afternoon went with him. How tall Bruce had grown in the last few years! How strong and caring, even more than when she had been small.

"He's better than any brother could be," she told a dandelion puff, then watched it fly into the still air. A feeling that someday she and Bruce would be tossed and torn apart the same way made her shiver. "Silly me. Nothing can change Bruce." Her smile returned and her blue eyes shone. Of course she'd miss her pal but time would go by rapidly and he'd be home for vacations. Mother and Dad had promised to take her to Seattle sometimes, too, so they could see the boy who had practically grown up in their home after his mother died.

Candleshine kept that smile all through his leaving and the years that followed. She also studied hard and graduated as valedictorian of her class. As her valedictory address she chose the subject, "Hold High the Torch," and triumphantly ended with a challenge to her fifteen classmates — and herself.

"We can refuse to carry on all that is good and worthwhile," her voice rang, "yet dare we?" She paused before continuing. "King David, a man of great wisdom, once said, 'For thou wilt light my candle: the Lord my God will enlighten my darkness.'* While we rejoice on the completion of our high school days this beautiful May 1938 afternoon, dictators are rending China, Spain, Austria, and many other countries. The darkness of war cannot help but touch us in many ways and only the lighted candles of our lives can help lift the smothering blackness creeping over the world.

"I will be eighteen in December. In January I begin training to become a nurse. I intend to follow Florence Nightingale's bright example. It doesn't matter *how* we keep our torches burning, but that we do. Together, we can create an everlasting flame." She stumbled back to her place amid loud cheering and the satisfied, proud

*Psalm 18:28 (KJV).

looks she received from her parents and Bruce, who had somehow wangled time off from his studies and ward work to attend this milestone in her life.

Summer, a busy time for all, seemed to fly. Candleshine took over complete charge of household duties so her mother could return to Bellingham for summer school before going back to teaching after so many years. She sang as she cooked, secretly delighted at her father's eager acceptance of meals and help with haying.

Fall became a waiting time to be put to rest by a joyous celebration on the twentieth of December. A combination eighteenth birthday and farewell party left Candleshine understanding how a wishbone must feel when pulled two ways. Through teary eyes she thanked family and friends and assured them her body would be in Seattle but much of her heart would always be in Cedar Ridge.

In the first week of January 1939 Candace Thatcher presented herself to the Mercy Hospital School training office and discovered Superintendent of Nurses Miss Genevieve Grey. Her shiny, steel-drill eyes, which perfectly matched her equally efficient hair, saw right through probationers. Candleshine shivered as she recalled Bruce telling her some classmates would be weeded out in the first three probationary months before being accepted as a student nurse. Common sense came to her rescue. No one could be better prepared and again she silently thanked God and Bruce for their help. She also determined she would *not* be dismissed. Bolstered, she met the keen gray gaze and found compassion, fairness, and even a twitch of humor in Miss Grey's stoic face.

After a jumble of corridors that might be harder to learn than bones, Candleshine stumbled through the covered passage that led from the School of Nursing to Hunter Hall, the two-story red brick nurses residence that matched the various hospital buildings sprawled on a hill above Seattle.

"Probationers and first-year students on the first floor, second year, seniors, and graduates on the second." Dark-haired, dark-eyed Winona Allen, who proudly admitted junior status, took Candleshine upstairs before showing the newcomer her own room.

"Why?"

Winona stared. Although Candace had to look down a few inches at her guide, she felt dwarfed until a mischievous look led to a whisper.

"Don't let it get around but it's so probies and first years won't sneak out. No one gets past good ol' housemom." She grinned. "Juniors and seniors are supposed to be past all that. Besides, when we have night duty it's quieter upstairs."

This time Candleshine bit her lip and didn't blurt out another stupid question. As she meekly followed Winona to her own room on first floor, Winona announced she looked forward to being the Cedar Ridge girl's Big Sister. Although it little resembled her wallpapered, comfortable bedroom at home, Candleshine rejoiced that her spotless window framed a view of Puget Sound.

"I lived in this room last year," Winona said. "You get some spectacular sunsets over the water."

Excitement blended with shyness. "I-Im glad you're my Big Sister."

"So am I. If you ever need a shoulder to cry on — and you will, we all do — I'll be here." An unexpectedly sweet smile replaced the elfish grin. "Welcome, Candace Thatcher, or is it Candy?"

She hesitated. *Would Winona think her nickname silly?*

"It's — Candleshine."

"That's lovely and how fitting for a nurse! Just don't let your light go out when you drop a bedpan or a doctor yells." For a moment doubt crossed her face. "You're really strong, aren't you? Nurses have to be."

"Strong enough to lift hay bales and drive a tractor."

"Good!" Winona glanced at her watch. "Oh, you have an hour before dinner. Better study the thou-shalt-nots."

"I beg your pardon?"

"Those." Winona nodded toward the list of rules conspicuously posted on the inside of the door. "And that." She indicated a framed motto next to it. "Probationer's supper is at six-thirty. Someone will be in the living room here to take you over. See you later, I have to go." She left the door open when she went out. "Friendlier this way."

How lucky to have this vivacious nurse for her Big Sister! "Thank You, God," she prayed before examining the forbidding list.

None was unfamiliar. Bruce had already warned her of the rules in "his" hospital — no jewelry, no eating on wards, no accepting invitations from doctors, no visiting wards except when on duty or sent by a superior, and one must always rise for doctors or higher ranking nurses.

"Yes, Doctor Thatcher." Candleshine bobbed an absurd curtsy and came upright to face a slight, smiling girl who stood giggling in the hall.

"Hello!" Candleshine stepped aside. "Won't you come in? I'm Candace Thatcher but everyone calls me Candleshine. Are you new, too?" she added hopefully.

"Very. I'm Constance Imoto, Connie to you. I came yesterday."

"I see you survived Miss Grey." Candleshine clapped her hand to her mouth but relaxed when Connie laughed and said, "Barely!"

By the time they were escorted to supper Candleshine knew God had sent a friend. Afterward when they strolled on the park-like grounds in the unusually warm January evening and Connie gazed at the lights of Seattle and whispered, "I thank God I am able to come here," Candleshine rejoiced. Imagine finding a fellow Christian the first day of training! Connie said her Japanese-American family had been shocked when she'd accepted Jesus after a high school friend witnessed of God's love. Now she prayed for her Shinto* family.

Connie was born of *nisei* Japanese parents, that is, children of immigrants born or

*A principal religion of Japan based on the worship of nature and of ancestors.

18

educated in the United States. "I look Japanese and think American," she shared. She never tired of hearing stories about Cedar Ridge and how Will and Trinity took one look at one another and fell in love. By the end of the week both girls looked forward to visiting the other's home if they could have time off together.

They also served to inspire each other's best. Candleshine's knowledge of anatomy complemented Connie's deft bedmaking and together they shared honors in physiology. Connie hated bandaging and Candleshine secretly rejoiced in the times she'd worked with Bruce on the ranch when animals got hurt. Connie acted a little awed that her new friend was a cousin of the much-respected Doctor Thatcher who sent ripples through the entire student nurse population!

As juniors and seniors the girls participated in the wide variety of training necessary before taking state exams and earning their coveted R.N. (Registered Nurse) status. They also made mistakes. None tragic, but a few disheartening enough for Candleshine to seek out faithful Winona until she graduated with honors.

Suddenly the hectic pace increased even more. Decisions must be made on what type of nursing to do when graduated. Dr. Bruce Thatcher and a team of specially selected nurses, including Winona, won the chance to work and learn in a hospital in Manila, the Philippines. Now thousands of miles would separate Bruce and Candleshine, yet through the rest of her training his parting admonition to always keep her light shining for their God steadied her. The year-long assignment would fly, then Bruce would return. Winona wasn't so certain of her future. After the peacetime draft in September 1940, the dedicated nurse's childhood sweetheart enlisted and later was stationed in Hawaii with the U.S. Pacific Fleet.

When Winona told the girls goodbye, her snappy dark eyes glistened. "I must be crazy. The Philippines are even farther from Hawaii than Seattle." She shrugged. "Oh, well, maybe one of us can get leave. It's been months since I saw him."

"I think it's exciting," Candleshine told her. "If you weren't already engaged, I'd love to have you for a cousin-in-law."

"If I weren't already 'spoken for' as my grandmother persists in calling it, I wouldn't mind at all," Winona shot back.

Weeks grew into months until just a short time remained until graduation. Candleshine and Connie still hadn't settled on how and where they could best use their skills, although both had prayed fervently. When Candleshine had a long weekend in early December, Will Thatcher came for his daughter and proudly escorted her to the car. Trinity had elected to have dinner ready for a family she knew from experience would be starving after the long drive from Seattle to Cedar Ridge.

Saturday offered total relaxation, a dusting of snow, and more peace and quiet than Candleshine could ask. She had a long talk with her parents that evening, discussing Bruce and her future. She needed an island of rest before the final, hard pull to shore that marked the end of her training.

The next day the world exploded, made even more horrible by the contrast with the calm such a few hours earlier. Japanese planes had bombed Pearl Harbor at the same time Japanese ambassadors were meeting with Secretary of State Cordell Hull. The world sat stunned, except for Candleshine.

"Mother, Dad, I must go back." Every tiny freckle stood out against her pale skin. "I'll be needed, especially by Connie. Oh, how could this evil thing happen?"

Millions of people asked the same question. The next day President Roosevelt officially declared war on Japan. So did Canada and Great Britain. On 9 December China declared war on the Rome–Berlin–Tokyo Axis. Germany and Italy retaliated on 11 December by declaring war on the United States. Christmas 1941, in the midst of World War II, truly a global conflict, would be bleak.

Now Candleshine fought unspeakable battles. Not against sickness and death but against the sidelong glances, sneers, and unfriendly comments a few of her classmates directed at both Connie and herself. "How can they?" she cried one day when she and Connie discovered signs on the doors of their Hunter Hall rooms. Connie's read, *"TRAITOR,"* while Candleshine's read, *"JAP-LOVER."*

Candleshine ripped the signs down and tore them to bits while dissolving into angry tears the way she hadn't done since childhood. "You're an American, more loyal than anyone I know. So are your parents." She thought of the gracious Imotos and the way they had welcomed her. She thought of Connie's older brother who had raced to enlist the moment he heard news of the attack.

"Some people will always be afraid of what is different," Connie said quietly. "They do not know God is colorblind."

Trust and faith shone in the smaller

woman's face and Connie wordlessly gripped Candleshine's hands, then entered her own room and shut the door.

A dozen times Candleshine walked by little knots of nurses who looked down when she passed, especially if Connie were with her. Gradually the hostile atmosphere depressed even the brave Japanese-American. "I won't quit after I've come so far," she said as she fingered a package Candleshine had wrapped for home. "Perhaps the Christmas spirit of peace will help."

Both women were on duty Christmas Eve. Candleshine swallowed back her disappointment. She hadn't been home for Christmas since before entering training. Neither had Connie. They had put aside their own longings and volunteered to work and relieve nurses with families.

For the third time they joined the serpentine procession of white-clad nurses who marched through the halls carrying candles and singing timeless carols of hope and joy and peace. Candleshine saw those blessings in Connie's face and gave thanks, although her vision blurred until the many flames dimmed. . . .

The long line of seniors, juniors, and probationers reached the end of the hall separating the graduates from training and duty. Candleshine returned to the present from a past that blended faith and fear, joy and love, and tragedy.

Again she looked at Connie who walked beside her in friendship and faith, more serious than ever before.

Candleshine shivered. The day they had so eagerly anticipated had dawned, but to scowling, dark skies that prophesied an uncertain future.

Two

Three years ago Connie Imoto's appearance in the hall outside Candleshine's room interrupted the Cedar Ridge probie's study of the thou-shalt-nots and turned her attention from the framed motto beside it. Yet during those years both girls had memorized the motto.

Nursing is an art; and if it is to be made an art, it requires as exclusive a devotion, as hard a preparation, as any painter's or sculptor's work; for what is the having to do with dead canvas or cold marble, compared with having to do with the living body — the temple of God's spirit? It is one of the Fine Arts. I had almost said, the finest of the Fine Arts.

Florence Nightingale

Now at graduation the framed charge

graced one side of the large room. On the other hung the beautiful Florence Nightingale Pledge. At the end of graduation the nurses rose as a body and repeated the timeless vow. Never had Candleshine felt so strongly about her chosen profession as when hushed voices in the room lit only by symbolically lighted lamps promised before God and those assembled to pass their lives in purity, practice their profession faithfully, and dedicate themselves.

Candleshine choked and fought back tears. She could see wet faces around her. Even the most irresponsible young women who had barely made it through training obviously grasped the significance of the moment.

Miss Grey, spotless as usual, dismissed the assembly in a ragged voice far from her usual disciplined timbre. "Sister Elizabeth Kinney said it far better than I when she spoke in truth and beauty the words, 'There is no profession that so closely follows in the footsteps of Christ, than the work of healing.' Go. Serve. And make Mercy Hospital and Training School proud to name you as our own."

A mighty wave of applause accompanied the dignified Superintendent's hasty exit from the platform, but not before those gathered saw her twisted face and glistening eyes.

Candleshine felt her heart swell with pride and pain. The petty irritations at classmates and staff and even the strenuous work faded into bonds that would hold no matter what came. She felt Connie's small but strong fingers dig into her arm and knew her friend felt the same way.

"I wonder — a year from now — where will we be?" Connie whispered.

"I'll be overseas." Candleshine set her lips in a grim line that aged her face. "I've already asked Miss Grey to let me stay on in the casualty ward. It will be good training." She looked deep into her friend's dark eyes. "What about you?"

"I, too, will stay here for the present." Connie's lips trembled and a curious paleness flooded her smooth skin.

Candleshine impulsively hugged her friend. "No matter how far apart we may be, it won't make a difference. Our hearts will stay close."

"Always." Connie drew in an unsteady breath. "I have thanked God everyday since I came for your friendship and love."

Too filled to speak, Candleshine nodded and quickly turned from the pain in Connie's face. "Dad, Mom — are you proud?"

Trinity seized her daughter and Will beamed on both girls impartially.

"Glad I became a nurse?"

Will cocked his head to one side and his blue eyes sparkled with fun. "Well, seems I remember you two moaning that until you passed state exams you wouldn't really be nurses."

"We intend to pass them with honors," his daughter boasted, but her blue eyes darkened. "It's more important now than ever." She ran one hand over her misty gaze. "I just wish Bruce and Winona could be here. Who knows what is happening in Manila?"

"Now that General MacArthur's forces have abandoned Manila and withdrawn to the Bataan Peninsula, communications will be terrible," said Will impassively, yet his worry for the boy closer than a son was etched in crisscross lines on his face.

"Bruce and Winona will never leave unless they're ordered out," Candleshine said. Visions of her laughing cousin and Big Sister who had guided her through early training days engulfed her. An urge to smash through the helplessness brought an agonized cry, "Oh, if there were only something we could do!"

"Our job is to pass our tests, become Registered Nurses, and wait," Connie reminded. "And pray."

"I know." She slowly unclenched her fingers.

"Think of Winona," Connie continued, her eyes enormous in her small face. "Her fiancé was stationed in Hawaii. He may have been killed."

"Connie's right." Trinity's blue eyes so like her daughter's did more to calm Candleshine than anything. "The same God we trusted before all this is still in control." She even managed a little smile. "Our part is simply to do the work we are given and, as Connie says, pray." She glanced at Will.

Candleshine caught the look. Would she one day look at a special man with the same love and trust in her mother's face? Her mouth set in a straight, unnatural line. Not until this hellish war ended. She could barely stand knowing Bruce was in danger. If she had a husband or fiancé off fighting . . . she refused to finish the thought. Not even for the precious love she had been privileged to witness in her home would she risk the certain torture of love in wartime.

To their surprise, the next afternoon Connie and Candleshine both received summonses to Miss Grey's office. The Superintendent had little of the starch associated with her demeanor except for her pressed uniform and ever-present cap. The steel-drill eyes looked liquid gray and compassion flowed from her. "Candace, I have bad news for you."

She hesitated and added, "That's why I asked Constance to come with you."

"Bruce?" Candleshine felt the blood drain from her face. She stared at Miss Grey, a tower of strength in a shaking world.

"We do not know that either Dr. Thatcher or Winona Allen have been harmed," Miss Grey continued. "We do know Manila has fallen. On January second Japanese forces took control of the city."

"The hospital? The staff?"

"No word is yet available, Candace." Miss Grey leaned forward and some of the steel returned to her eyes. "If Dr. Thatcher could send you a message right now it would be to not let this news keep you from doing your duty."

"Duty!" Candleshine didn't know whether to laugh or cry.

"Yes, duty. You once told me Dr. Thatcher's dream was for you to become a nurse. Nothing must interfere with that. *Nothing.*" Only Miss Grey's tightly clasped hands betrayed the woman behind the dedicated administrator.

"I — I don't know if I can."

"You must and you will. Constance, see that Candleshine gets a brisk afternoon walk. I've arranged for you to have the rest of the day off. Walk her until she can barely stumble back, then eat and get her to bed." She turned and gazed out the window into a Seattle sky as gray as her eyes. "I find that prescription works when I falter." She stood and added, "You may go."

Only later did the young women remember that for the first of a very few times Miss Grey used Nurse Thatcher's nickname.

With the spunk of her pioneering ancestors, Candleshine obeyed Miss Grey. When the clouds of war hovered, she forced herself to ignore them and rejoiced when every single class member passed the state exams. Many, like the two friends, elected to get extra training until accepted by the army, navy, or Red Cross. Never had the work been more grueling for those remaining of the class of '42. Grim-lipped but with a forced cheerfulness — not only for the patients' sake but what their skilled hands would someday be required to do — the nurses bonded and served.

One good thing came from the long

hours: The prejudice against Connie Imoto dwindled. No one could see the way she drove herself and not respect her. She would need every ounce of her strength and endurance to withstand what lay ahead.

In mid-February Miss Grey called the two nurses in again. She sat with her head in her hands for a time before speaking. Finally she raised a haggard face. "Nurse Imoto, Constance —" she spread her hands helplessly. "Dear God. . . ." Not a curse, but a prayer.

Connie clutched Candleshine's arm until the taller nurse wanted to scream with pain, "Is it my parents?"

Her terror penetrated Miss Grey's abstraction. "No, no, child. Not your brother, either." She wordlessly pointed to a message on her desk. "President Roosevelt has signed the Japanese Relocation Order."

"But what does that have to do with Connie?" Candleshine burst out, for once unafraid of her superior's attitude. "Connie and her parents are *Americans!*"

"I know." Miss Grey's control gradually returned. "In times of war fear dictates strange happenings."

"What is it?" Connie whispered.

"In simple terms, West Coast Japanese

persons will be sent to designated military relocation centers to avoid any possibility of espionage."

"*Espionage? Connie?*" Candleshine wanted to laugh. "Who in his right mind would think Connie or her parents could be spies?"

"It is also for the protection of Japanese and Japanese-Americans," Miss Grey said soberly. "There have already been a few incidents of rock throwing and the Ku Klux Klan is said to be burning crosses and threatening people. These are isolated incidents, probably by individual fanatics rather than organized groups, but enough to cause concern."

Connie moistened her dry lips. "Wh— where will we be sent?"

"It's too soon to tell," Miss Grey said.

"Can't you do anything?" Candleshine pleaded.

"I will do everything in my power," Miss Grey promised. "But Constance, I doubt that even the strongest recommendations on the part of Mercy Hospital will prevent your relocation."

Youth died in her face. She stood erect, her shoulders squared. The woman within spoke proudly. "I would not accept anything else. I must go with my family."

Candleshine made a muffled, hurting sound and Connie turned to her.

"Please don't. Didn't we vow to serve wherever we might be? Think of the need I will find in a camp. Sickness knows no boundaries." Pity for her friend drowned out possible fear and anguish. "One day the war will end. Until then —" She gallantly raised her head and smiled. "I will serve in the place my God has allowed me to be."

Connie slowly walked across the room, opened the door, and slipped through.

Candleshine made a move to follow her, awed by the radiance in Connie's whole body.

"No, Candace. Let her pride remain intact. Only God can see your friend through the next moments. Let Him work before you go to her."

By night every person at Mercy Hospital and Training School knew the situation. Almost unanimously they agreed to approach their department heads, supervisors, and even the hospital board of directors. Not once did Candleshine see a glimmer of triumph or gladness over Connie's misfortune.

"I can take that with me," Connie told her when she left the hospital. In a few days she and her family and hundreds of others would be transported to a relocation center, perhaps Tule Lake in northern California or Minidoka in Idaho. How could she face the barbed wire and guards Candleshine heard surrounded the barren camps?

"My brother is fighting somewhere far worse than where I will be," Connie said immediately. "We don't even know where, just that he's been shipped out. We won't be mistreated or starved. Candleshine, there are many ways to fight and win a war. Our United States of America *will* fight. We *will* win. That's what I hang onto."

Candleshine never mentioned it again.

Connie's absence from Mercy Hospital left a gaping hole. Yet the increased tempo since 7 December kept even Candleshine from more than temporary mourning. She volunteered for extra duty; she worked as if the entire outcome of the war rested on her slim but capable shoulders. She prayed constantly and often sang small patients to sleep when all the formal care and medications in the world could not soothe. From casualty to surgery, pediatrics to medical she went, rejoicing in the splendid strength God had given her to serve beyond her own capacity. Little by little doctors, patients, and even Miss Grey dropped the more formal "Candace" or "Nurse Thatcher" and called her by her well-chosen nickname.

One usually grumpy surgeon said all that Thatcher woman had to do was walk on a ward and patients brightened up.

At times the war seemed far away. When President Roosevelt ordered General Mac-Arthur to Australia from Bataan in March after three heartsick months of repelling the Japanese despite malnutrition and disease, a new feeling of dread was sparked. MacArthur's promise to the Filipinos, "I shall return," gained instant notoriety and enlisted sympathy for the cause.

Candleshine went on with her home-front battle against sickness and accidents. Not one word had been heard from either Bruce or Winona since before Christmas. The name of Winona's fiancé had appeared in the "killed in action" lists from the attack on Pearl Harbor.

Newspapers faithfully followed the war's progress and no amount of pretense could keep patients from getting copies. Candleshine learned to know in those endless weeks how things were going by the morale on her wards when she arrived. The staff looked the other way when excited patients on the less serious wards pulled tricks after any bit of good news. Bad news brought an even greater measure of tenderness toward those with "boys over there."

Candleshine heard herself reassure many a faded mother, "God can care for your boy in the Pacific theater as well as here at home." How many quiet prayers did she offer when gnarled hands or burly, ashamed shoulders shook with agony?

The morning of 9 April 1942, Candleshine awoke to a feeling of foreboding reinforced by total exhaustion. She had been on an extra-long duty the night before. She discovered the courageous 75,000 wornout troops had finally surrendered Bataan to the Japanese. Stories hit the press of a sixty-five-mile march — Americans as prisoners of war were forced to march to Japanese prison camps — with many deaths on the way due to disease and mistreatment.

Had Bruce been part of the so-called Bataan Death March? Had Winona? Candleshine shuddered and called on God for courage before going back on duty.

Japan would not be safe for long. On 18 April 1942, Lieutenant Colonel James "Jimmy" Doolittle led sixteen B-25 bombers from the flight deck of the aircraft carrier *Hornet* more than 600 miles and raided Tokyo and other Japanese cities. Although the attack did little damage, the shock value reverberated in the hearts of a waiting people and rocked Japanese confidence. The expression, "We did it once — we can do it again," rang through Mercy Hospital.

And still Candleshine waited. Her parents trembled when she took her stand and said she'd go overseas as soon as she could. Yet even as Will and Trinity shared sleepless nights praying for their daughter and Bruce, Winona, Connie, and all the other young men and women caught in the war, they clung to each other and to their God.

"We cannot order her what to do," Will said brokenly. Yet pride streaked his face.

Not even the miscarriage of their first child brought suffering to match Trinity's exquisite pain, a pain evident in the new white gracefully blended into her dark locks. First Bruce, then Candleshine. Yet on the few occasions she and Will had to see Candleshine, Trinity kept things light except for that final, penetrating look that said more than she could speak.

Weeks droned by until in May the Battle of the Coral Sea, in which neither side ever saw the other's ships but fought only by planes sent from aircraft carriers, halted the threat to Australia.

When the first of the returning wounded began to arrive, Candleshine requested exclusive duty on the wards now set apart for them. Grizzled and middle-aged men, boys scarcely out of their teens, together their indomitable spirits pulled them through against incredible odds. Deeds of bravery and reports of trivial incidents mingled. But all the men had one thing in common: They wanted to rest, heal, see their families, *and go back.*

One normally profane sergeant who successfully curbed his tongue in the presence of the nurses said it all in one sentence: "The job ain't done and 'til it is, I gotta be there." In vain Candleshine tried to convince him he'd given all that was required, including three fingers of his left hand when a grenade misfired.

"Little gal, you an' others like you won't never be safe while Tojo-devils are runnin' loose," he said, patting her hand with his good right one. "I still have two good legs and one good hand, don't I?"

She didn't have the heart to tell him she doubted he'd be sent back to the Pacific theater with a deformed left hand. The day new orders came and she ripped them open for him, Candleshine admired this rough man more than ever. A black shade dropped over his face. He swallowed hard, lifted his chin, and stared into her eyes as if daring her to disagree with him.

"Guess what, nurse! They're gonna give me a medal an' take advantage of all my smarts. Soon as you let me out of here I've got me a new job right here in the good old U.S. of A. I get to herd new, ignorant guys around at Fort Lewis an' show them how to be real soldiers."

"Good for you. No one can do it better," she flashed back at him and the entire ward cheered.

But that night long after low groans betrayed troubled dreams, Candleshine's quick ears caught a muffled sobbing. She hurried to the tough sergeant's bed and without a word, gripped his good hand with her own. He hung on for dear life. The sobs dwindled, then stopped.

"Think I'm a baby?" The shamed, broken whisper pierced Candleshine's soul. It could be Bruce lying in the darkness, hiding his feelings from others.

"No, sergeant." Her low voice stilled him and he let go of her hand. "Remember, things always look brighter in the morning." She deliberately switched from comforter to efficient nurse, smoothed his pillow, bathed his hot face, and brought fresh water. "God bless."

"An' you." A final, convulsive sound told her the storm had ended.

A few days later he moved on, one of an endless line of soldiers, sailors, and fliers who claimed Candleshine's attention and care for a season before continuing on the human conveyor belt to fight again, some back overseas, many at home.

In early June America again rejoiced, this time over the first major Allied victory in the Battle of Midway. By taking out four of Japan's nine aircraft carriers, the enemy's naval power was crippled. Slowly the terrible tide of aggression had begun to turn. Yet America fell to its knees again when a few days later Japan seized two islands at its own back door, at the tip of the Alaskan Aleutian chain.

One summer evening Candleshine turned from sickness and war news to the solace of a warm, inviting evening overlooking Puget Sound. Gold-touched waves from a setting sun lapped the beach clearly visible from the weary nurse's window. The forested slopes of Bainbridge Island brought a homesick longing for Cedar Ridge. *Would their family ever be intact there again?*

Candleshine threw wide the window, unwilling to be separated from the evening even by a single pane of glass. All the heartache, worry, and struggles loosened their bindings for a single moment.

A feeling this could be one of the last times she stood at the window touched her. Not a premonition, but a thought. God had left her at Mercy Hospital to learn many lessons. Now she believed the time to move on loomed near, even as the ferry boat coming across the sound grew larger.

She suddenly remembered what Bruce said long ago when she held the squirming yellow cat for "Dr. Thatcher's" bandaging.

"Knowing this — and your folks and mine — will always be here to come back to makes it easier for me to go. . . ."

"God, may this peaceful, beautiful part of your creation continue free," she prayed. The last ray of daylight hovered on the horizon as one star appeared. Comforted, Candleshine watched the velvet night descend and cherished the moment.

Three

While Candleshine drove herself and chafed at the waiting, a world away Bruce Thatcher and Winona Allen struggled against unspeakable odds to practice their skills. The tall brown-haired doctor and the petite, bubbly nurse worked as smoothly together as two blades on a pair of shears. A warm friendship based on mutual love for Candleshine and home sprang up between them. In addition Bruce offered the solid security of his personality and position: After only a few weeks at Manila Hospital the quality of Bruce's work was evident.

The bombing of Pearl Harbor and the landing of the first Japanese troops in the Philippines three days later presented a grave problem for the medical team from the States. Should they stay or ask to be evacuated?

"If we wait, we may not get out later,"

Bruce warned his fellow workers. "Winona, what about you?"

Her dark eyes flashed while her short black curls bobbed in a defiant gesture. "I stay."

"And I."

"Same here."

Not one of the team agreed to leave, even when an influx of wounded sent the entire hospital scrambling to provide care. Supplies ran low. Although red-eyed from lack of sleep, the only thing that kept the staff going was the knowledge they made a difference.

More and more Winona turned to Bruce for strength. The first time a badly hurt Japanese soldier lay helplessly waiting for the aid she could offer, Winona cringed. While she proceeded to give the best care she could, a half-hour later Dr. Thatcher found her crying in a linen closet.

"How can I take care of those — those —" She broke off, but her anger, despair, and guilt still raged within.

Bruce didn't say a word. He just gathered the small nurse into his strong, brotherly arms and waited.

"I — I keep th— thinking that maybe a b— brother or c— cousin was one of those at P— Pearl Harbor," she sobbed. "One who helped b— bomb our fleet a— and. . . ."

Before she could pronounce her deepest fears involving her fiancé Bruce said, "I feel the same way."

She jerked away from him, stunned by his quiet words. "Then h— how c— can you — ?"

Bruce's poignant blue eyes looked deep into Winona's. " 'Inasmuch as ye have done it unto one of the least of these my brethren, ye have done it unto me.' "* Bruce's jaw was set. "I repeat this over and over." He smiled at Winona. "I can't say I don't still rebel but it helps me put aside my own feelings to see a hurting human being instead of a fallen enemy."

Chastened and humbled, Winona murmured, "I wish I had your faith."

"I've seen you do things only Christ could do as far as compassion," Bruce told her huskily. "You told me you accepted Him long ago."

"I did." Winona groped for a handkerchief and blew her nose. "Maybe I'm just so filled with anger at all this unnecessary dying and misery I can't concentrate on Jesus." Her unsinkable spirits rose.

*Matthew 25:40 (KJV).

"Thanks, pal, I mean, Dr. Thatcher. I can go on now."

That evening Bruce saw Winona bending over a dying Japanese soldier no older than herself. Every trace of hatred had vanished and her worn face shone like a flower in the overcrowded ward.

A few days later when Manila's capture was imminent, Bruce, Winona, and the others were taken to the Bataan Peninsula. Common sense had driven them away over protests. Winona would never forget the midnight trip in a small boat painted black against detection. Incredible as it seemed, they got through, due to the skill of the Filipino fisherman who knew the waters as well as he knew himself.

The beginning of 1942 saw the team in a hastily constructed tent hospital. The anguish a few days later when news came that Manila had fallen left Winona feeling the world had turned upside down. To a nurse born in Seattle where winter rains and snow now fell, January in Bataan with its mild temperatures, continual enemy attacks, and privation added to her confusion. Too tired to do more than grimace, she went on with her work.

Malnutrition and disease added to the general misery. "It's bad enough just trying to care for the wounded," Winona told Bruce. "But *this!*" Their encampment, camouflaged as much as possible against the enemy, provided little defense against hunger and sickness.

"Are you taking your Atabrine? Every day?" he demanded. "The last thing we need is for you — or any of us — to come down with malaria."

"I take it." The corners of her mouth turned down. "Can't you tell by my beautiful yellow complexion?"

He managed a tired grin. "Better than malaria."

"Barely." But she reluctantly responded to his teasing. Not often did humor touch any of their lives these days. And she faithfully continued with her Atabrine. She might joke about malaria but the thought of it left her weak. Every pair of able hands must be available to work.

At times Winona and Bruce felt time meant nothing: a few hours' sleep, then back to duty, with insufficient food hastily wolfed down when time permitted, and always the threat of attack. Weeks limped by. Late in March the commander of the camp called the United States team aside.

"We can't hold out much longer. We've beaten back Japanese attacks for three months but we can't go on. Too much sickness, not enough food and manpower." He wiped his sweaty face. "You have to go." He ignored the wave of protest. "You'll be taken to Corregidor — tonight. It's all arranged."

They stared. Corregidor, the rocky, fortified island at the entrance of Manila Bay on the island of Luzon, held large caves. United States and Filipino troops had dug in and continued to defend it.

The weary commander silenced their protests. "It's my hope they can hold out on Corregidor longer than we can here, at least long enough to get you away."

"But there's no guarantee." Steel laced Bruce's statement.

"None."

"Then why should we go?" Winona exploded. "I won't. Even with everything every one of us can do we can't begin to handle the ocean of patients pouring in. How can you expect to get by without us?" Her clear voice rang in the suddenly silent room. "Every one of us pledged to serve where needed, as do military personnel." Her voice broke for a moment, the way it had done when they finally received word her fiancé had been killed at Pearl Harbor. The next instant she proudly finished. "Excuse me, commander, but if our meeting is over I have work to do on the ward. May I go?"

Winona held her breath. *Had she gone too far in making her point?* Doubt clutched her throat. *Maybe they should go to Corregidor. Those rock caves promised at least temporary security.*

No. If the God she had grown close to in this continuing fight against death wanted her to live, nothing could happen. If not — she shrugged. She had seen too much dying to fear it, especially when she knew with all her heart physical death would not be the end for her or Bruce or any who believed in the saving power of their Lord.

Perhaps something of her inner acceptance showed in her face. The commander peremptorily waved toward the door. "Dismissed, Nurse Allen. What about the rest of you?"

Before she got to the door Winona heard her team's unanimous promise to stick together no matter what happened.

If some team members later regretted the decision, only God knew. They doubled and tripled their efforts until one fateful day when Winona fell asleep on her feet and dropped a precious bottle of medicine.

"That's it," Bruce ordered, his heart torn by his friend's stubborn refusal to quit. He seized her by the shoulders and faced her toward the ward door. "Go to bed and stay there until you wake up naturally."

She managed a feeble grin, a shadow of her former smile. "Okay, boss. We can't afford to lose any more medicine." She shook her head to clear it for the short walk to a nearby tent that housed the nurses after an enemy bomb leveled their former quarters. Too tired to get out of her disheveled, soiled uniform, she fell on her hard cot, pulled a rough blanket over her head to diminish the sounds of bombing in the distance, and slept.

Hours later she awakened to Bruce's fierce shake and chilling orders. "Get up. We have to get out!" He shook her again, hard, his medical bag in his other hand.

Refreshed by sleep, Winona's body and mind responded to the urgency in his voice. "What is it?"

"Our troops have surrendered. They had no choice." Bruce's haggard face showed no surprise but an acceptance of the inevitable. "We're going to make a break and see if we can get to Corregidor. Don't wait to take anything, just come!"

If the midnight trip to Bataan had been a nightmare, their flight to Corregidor made it seem like a Sunday school picnic. Still wearing her messy uniform and clinging to Bruce's strong arm, Winona stumbled with her protector, glad for her renewed strength. She and Bruce raced through shell-pocked ground until both gasped for breath. Once Bruce stopped, clutched Winona's hand, and whispered, "We've done all we can, God. Now we're in Your hands."

From the prayer came endurance beyond belief that lent courage to go on long past human will.

Of those who fled to Corregidor, only a few made it. A dozen times Winona's heart leaped until she felt smothered. Only silent prayers and the nearness of Bruce Thatcher kept her huddled and quiet. Even when they drifted to an apparently uninhabited bit of Corregidor shore and ran for cover after intently scanning the terrain, Winona crouched beneath Bruce's protective arm, too numb with shock to realize they had actually slipped past enemy territory. Hours later the Bataan refugees made contact with a nearby Allied unit. To Winona, the dirty and unshaven U.S. and Filipino soldiers looked like a platoon of angels.

"Begging your pardon, but we've a place for you," a kindly soldier told her. He led her deep into a cool cave and pointed to a corner. In the brief time since the newcomers' arrival someone had hung a frayed army blanket so she could have privacy.

All the tears Winona had held back so long rose inside her at such incongruous thoughtfulness in the middle of war. She blinked hard. "You have wounded. Where can I help most?"

"Dr. Thatcher says you're to rest first." The gruff order left no room for argument. "Sorry we can't offer you the Waldorf, but then, you look like you haven't been staying there lately anyway." His weathered lips split into a grin. He disappeared and a little later came back with a small basin of water, a canteen, and some food. "No hot and cold running water." He looked her up and down. "Hmmmm. Pretty dirty."

Again her self-appointed guardian vanished. Winona covered her mouth with her hand to keep from giggling when she heard his bellowing voice to his comrades.

"Hey, you guys, cough up some clothes for our visitor. She can't keep wearing that imported frock camouflaged as a uniform."

A loud cheer arose and a few minutes later the soldier came back in with khaki shirt and pants that, if not clean, were an improvement over her current clothing. "You'll have to roll up the sleeves and pant legs, even Shorty's a lot bigger than you."

"They'll be fine. Thank you and thank the men."

"We're honored."

American chivalry at its best, Winona thought. She bathed simply, ate the unappetizing but necessary food, and, with the help of a belt someone had considerately punched more holes in, dressed in her new apparel. A pallet in the corner invited. She'd sleep for just a few moments, then. . . .

Winona awoke to discover a comb, a toothbrush that smelled as if it had been dipped in some kind of disinfectant, and two pairs of socks more holey than righteous.

Once more tears crowded behind her eyelids but she ignored them, thanked God, and prepared to burst into the society of her new neighborhood.

The first person she met stared, then couldn't help exclaiming, "Haw, haw!"

Winona's lips turned up in sympathy. "I know. Isn't it awful?" In the dim light in her cave corner she couldn't see what she was doing. Now she surveyed her deeply turned up pant legs, one leg hanging down four inches longer than the other, and the bunched waist of the donated khakis. For the first time in weeks, her laugh rang out. It brought instant response from the soldiers who quickly gathered around her.

"Better than a tonic," one yelled. "That's what we've been needing around here. Some real, live, fashion model!"

Healing laughter echoed throughout the cave and Winona's spirits lifted.

"Do you feel ready to help me?" Bruce asked from the cave entrance.

Winona noted he had also been given fresh clothing, only his shirt didn't quite meet in front. Its donor must be much slimmer. "I'm ready." She trotted after him.

The pattern began that lasted for almost a month. Bruce beckoned, she followed. She learned to know and love the patients who eagerly turned to her, some even younger than herself. Her respect for Bruce deepened. How could he accomplish so much under such conditions?

One harrowing night Bruce literally saved a young Filipino soldier's life by performing a tracheotomy by flashlight. Afterward Winona thought of how many times Candleshine had talked about holding high a torch. *Would she and Bruce ever see her again?*

To the young nurse's surprise she discovered that although guns boomed and reverberated, fear waited to pounce and death surrounded her, "the peace that passeth understanding" never left her. Along with her deepening faith and devoted service, something else crept into Winona's life. Memory of her lost fiancé dulled with the passage of events she'd lived through and the daily necessity to go on. She realized one day while she'd never forget her first young love, she had the capacity to love again.

Sweeny, who doggedly claimed her as his girl " 'cause he took care of her when she first came" staked his claim. "Remember, guys. Hands off. When we get outa this dump and back home I'm going to come calling on Miss Winona Allen. When I wear my best blue serge, who can resist me?"

"You dumb guy, I bet Doc Thatcher will have something to say about that," someone called.

Sweeny spun toward the doctor. His eyes rounded and he exaggerated the awe in his voice. "That right, Doc?"

Winona felt red creep from her open shirt collar up into her face. *How would Bruce handle such joking? Maybe he'd be uncomfortable.*

Bruce didn't hesitate even for a heartbeat. He simply turned his blue gaze first on Winona's red face then toward Sweeny. "Sorry, buddy. When we get outa this dump

—" He mimicked Sweeny perfectly. "I'm going to come calling on Winona wearing my best white doctor's outfit." His grin lit up his thin face. "What nurse can resist a doctor?"

"Aw, Doc." Sweeny's face fell. "I'll be jiggered if I can hold out against you. Hey short stuff, do you have any sisters?"

She escaped to her corner, her face flaming. For hours she wondered why her long-frozen heart felt as if Bruce had indeed lighted a candle in its depths that left her warmed all over.

By 5 May the valiant Corregidor holdouts knew, in spite of everything they could do, the end lurked in the shadows. Bruce talked over with Winona what lay ahead.

"We'll be taken prisoner. I'm not sure where the Japanese will send us. Probably either to Santo Tomás internment camp or Bilibid prison. It's not going to be easy, Winona."

She knew the fear in his eyes was for her, not for himself. She sighed. "At least we missed the Bataan Death March." She shuddered, remembering the news gathered in bits and pieces through the limited contact with the outside world.

"The only way I can see that we may be spared at least a few of the indignities is to make much of our medical skills," Bruce said. "I wouldn't do it for myself." His lip curled. "For you —"

The poignant light that sometimes touched his blue eyes now filled them. Bruce gently took her hands. "Winona, I know it's too soon after Pearl Harbor and all that happened, but I meant what I told Sweeny. If, no, *when* we get home, would you open your door if a certain spiffed-up doctor knocked on it?"

A rush of emotion left her speechless. She could only nod.

Bruce left it at that. He squeezed her hands and whispered a broken "Try to rest" before leaving her alone with teary eyes and a hope that could never be extinguished.

The next day Japan claimed victory on Corregidor and the organized Allied resistance in the Philippines died.

Only Winona's faith in God and growing realization of her love for Bruce kept her from sheer insanity in the weeks and months that followed. True to Bruce's predictions, conditions in the internment camp proved sickening. His fervent pleas for the humane treatment guaranteed to prisoners of war under the Geneva Convention went unheeded. Treatment and care of the sick and wounded that was provided for in the Convention remained nonexistent. So did protection for civilians. Prisoners suffered from lack of food and existed on one small bowl of rice a day with now and then a few scraps of meat that Winona refused to identify for fear she could not get it down. As winter came, a lack of blankets and adequate covering against the tropical rains left many dead.

Winona fared slightly better only because Bruce proved of immeasurable value with his medical knowledge. Not that the guards cared for their prisoners. They treasured Dr. Thatcher's skills for the sake of themselves, but even that didn't help him escape all cruelty. When the men and women were separated into filthy barracks, Winona learned through the unstoppable line of communication how Bruce faced death.

The uniformed officers spotted the small caducean pin Bruce had managed to keep and proudly wore on his collar. "What is that?" they demanded.

"A symbol of my profession. I am a doctor."

"Silence!" One backhanded him and brought blood from his lips. "You are an American spy, sent to betray Japan."

"I am a doctor."

The soldier hit him again. "You are a spy."

Battered until almost senseless, Bruce knew he must convince them if he were to help Winona. His swollen lips continued to proclaim his profession until the guard threw him in a cell and left him there, evidently convinced this strong man spoke the truth.

A few days later the same guard jerked open the cell door, pulling Bruce out of a restless, troubled sleep, and ordered him to follow. Bruce stumbled back into the same room where he had been beaten. "If you are a doctor, fix him." The officer in charge pointed to a fellow officer on a cot in the corner who lay groaning and clutching his right side. Three minutes later Bruce knew he had one hot appendix to deal with — fast.

"I need help," he told the officer. "Bring Nurse Allen here."

"Impossible!" The officer glared and his thin eyebrows met in a scowl.

"Are you prepared to assist me?" Bruce's voice cut like a polished scalpel.

The officer on the cot wavered then ordered the guard, "Bring this nurse here."

Bruce lived a lifetime waiting for Winona. At least he would see her and know for himself how she fared. He would see in her eyes if she'd been mistreated.

Thank God, his heart cried when she came in, her eyes enormous with being summoned but untouched by horrors he'd imagined.

Less than an hour later Bruce and Winona had scrubbed in surprisingly hot water that had never made its way to the prisoners and Bruce made the incision.

Great beads of sweat stood on his forehead. If the appendix had burst or if peritonitis had set in, it meant his and Winona's deaths as well as the Japanese officer's. "Easy, now," he breathed, grateful for the small, skillful hands that had not lost their touch in the months of hardship.

"Now." He finished preliminary duties and with a lightning, trained motion removed the swollen, diseased appendix.

It burst in the pan.

"Sutures." Bruce stitched the wound as carefully as a woman sews her wedding dress and breathed a sigh of relief. He caught Winona's matching sigh with keen ears and whispered, "Praises be."

"No whispers. Guard, take the nurse away," the officer ordered.

"Thank you, Nurse Allen." Bruce's eyes said much more but her demure reply successfully hid from their persecutors how clearly she had received his message.

"Goodnight, Dr. Thatcher."

Her soft and eloquent look remained with Bruce long after he again lay in the wretched space allotted to him.

Four

"Nurse Thatcher?" A probationer still in her teens lightly tapped on Candleshine's open door.

"Yes?" Candleshine finished securing her cap and smiled at the hesitant young woman. How long it seemed since she had been a probie approaching her Big Sister's door. "Come in, Sally. How are you getting along?"

Sally Monroe stepped inside but shook her head when the older nurse motioned her to a chair. Her unruly red curls threatened to dislodge from the hairpins that restrained them. "Everything is fine, so far," she said. "Miss Grey would like to see you." Her brown eyes looked enormous. "Is it as scary to get called to her office when you're a real nurse as when you're a probie?"

Candleshine laughed, a joyous burst that relaxed Sally. "Almost." Her blue eyes twinkled. "Don't let Miss Grey frighten you,

Sally. She's one of the grandest women I've ever been privileged to know."

"I agree." Sally clasped her hands in earnestness and her entire face glowed. "It's just that when I see her I feel I must have done something wrong even when I know I didn't, if that makes any sense."

"It does. That's her way of getting the best from you." Candleshine hesitated then impulsively confessed, "Don't let it turn your head but Miss Grey thinks you show the most promise of anyone in your class."

"Oh, Miss Thatcher!" Red swept into the attractive face.

"That also means she will be harder on you than any other woman in your class," Candleshine warned.

"Think I care about that?" Sally squared her shoulders. "Thanks a trillion!" She swooped across the room, quickly kissed Candleshine's cheek, then fled, happy tears flowing.

"Was I ever that young?" Candleshine marveled then shrugged. "Probably, and far less sure of myself than Sally." She hastened downstairs, wrapped her cape close against the crisp winter air, and rapidly walked through the covered passage from Hunter Hall to the hospital and Miss Grey's office. Before entering, she idly fingered the letters

SUPERINTENDENT OF NURSES on the door. Could Miss Grey have the news that Candleshine had waited for so long, that would send her overseas? She breathed deeply and opened the door.

The first thing she noticed was Miss Grey's smile. The second, a soldier who leaned on a crutch and awkwardly got to his feet. She stifled the urge to tell him not to stand. Months ago she'd learned how much wounded soldiers resented being babied about their disabilities.

"Candace, this is Sergeant Sweeny." Miss Grey stood with a rustle of starched skirts and walked toward the door. "You may use my office for as long as you wish."

"Grand old dame, ain't she?" Sweeny commented almost before the door closed behind Miss Grey.

"I wouldn't exactly use those words, but yes, she's an excellent nurse and friend." Candleshine couldn't help laughing at the kindly but blunt sergeant. "How can I help you?"

"Sit down so I can." He settled back in his chair after she dropped to one nearby. "You're Bruce Thatcher's cousin, aren't you?"

Excitement washed through Candleshine and brought her out of her chair to kneel at

Sweeny's side. "How do you know? Where's Bruce? Is he all right? And Winona — Nurse Allen?"

Sergeant Sweeny grinned his crooked grin and his eyes shone then shadowed. "How long has it been since you heard from either of them?"

"Not since the fall of Manila."

Sweeny grunted in satisfaction. "Well, as of the sixth of May when Corregidor fell, your cousin and friend were alive and as well as could be expected, considering all things."

"Thank God!" Bright drops gathered but her hard-won discipline held them back. She blindly groped for Sweeny's hardened hand. "Tell me everything, please."

In brief sentences that allowed her to read far more between the lines than what he actually said, Sergeant Sweeny described the welcome arrival of "Doc" Thatcher and Nurse Winona. Candleshine laughed at his description of her short friend in khakis several sizes too large and rejoiced over the good the medical duo did on Corregidor. She held her breath when Sweeny continued.

"I know both of them were okay when we reached our new vacation hotel internment camp," Sweeny assured her. But his face wrinkled and he scowled. "Some dump."

He hurried on, obviously unwilling to go into details about the camp.

"Oh, Doc got in good with the head honchos by performing a neat little operation and saving one of them whose appendix went haywire. Your nurse friend helped." He threw back his head and laughed. "Can you believe I actually got down on my knees and gave thanks for that appendix?"

Candleshine couldn't even move. Her mind whirled. Bruce and Winona, incarcerated in a prison camp and still doing their medical best!

Sweeny's laughter died. "See, Doc traded on what he'd done and kept reminding the officers. Finally, probably to shut him up, they let him and Nurse Allen look after the worst hurt of the prisoners. They couldn't do a lot, but boy, they did a whole lot more than anyone could believe. Just having that pint-sized nurse walk into a filthy cell and grin that grin of hers shot morale out of the mud."

"How long ago was this?"

Sweeny scratched his head and stared out the window at the Seattle dusk. "Months."

"Sorry," he added, when Candleshine's head drooped. "Hey, they're going to be all right. That God of theirs won't let it be any other way."

So Bruce and Winona offered more than physical help, she thought.

"How did you get out?"

"Dug, at night. Thought we'd never make it." He licked his lips and Candleshine wished she hadn't asked.

"Five of us started. The guards got all but me." Anguish aged him. "I did all the things I learned as a kid. Waded when I could. Climbed trees. Finally, I made it to the middle of nowhere and they quit looking, I guess."

"What happened to your leg?"

"Took a bullet at Corregidor." A spasm of pain crossed his face. "If the Japanese hadn't finally let Doc look at it, I'd be missing my left leg. It kinda slowed me down when I got out but my buddies waited until I could walk pretty good." He shifted the leg. "Anyway, I hid out, pretty near starved, and met up with some Filipinos who'd escaped and hid in the hills. They took care of me." He closed his eyes and swallowed hard. "Say, if I hadn't believed in miracles before, I do now."

Candleshine tingled at his reverent voice and tightened her grip on the big man's hand.

"I wouldn't have thought an eel could get out of there but two Filipinos I'm proud to call brother snaked me through the jungle, stole a Japanese boat, knifed three guards, and appropriated their uniforms. I knew every inch of ocean we traveled would be our last."

His sudden, raucous laugh almost curled Candleshine's eyelashes. "We had enough trouble with the Japanese but when we got to where we had a chance of meeting up with our own troops, those darned prison uniforms near got us killed! I jerked off my T-shirt and waved it like a flag then started singing 'The Star-Spangled Banner' at the top of my lungs. It worked."

His breathless listener could almost see the vivid scene.

"Well, as soon as they could they got me picked up and taken to Australia. I spent some time in a hospital there — man, but those nurses are hardworking and pretty. One of them reminded me of your friend. . . ."

Disappointment filled Candleshine but she forced a bright smile. "I am so glad you came." Her lips quivered. "At least we can have hope for Bruce and Winona."

Sergeant Sweeny's face spread into a grin. Mischief danced in his eyes. "Think two people as much in love as those two need proper food and all that stuff? Didn't you ever hear about living on love?"

"Really? Are they really in love?"

Sweeny drew his mouth down in a fake frown. "Doc up and told me his intentions in front of everyone when I said I'd be calling on our little nurse after the war."

"What did Winona say?"

"Nothing. She just turned pink as the roses that climb into my window back home and headed for her own private bood-wahr in the corner of the cave." He looked wise. "They deserve each other. Besides, I've got someone writing to me and waiting until this mess is over, if her letters mean anything."

"I'm sure they do, sergeant," Candleshine softly told him. "I will never stop being thankful that you came."

He freed his hand and struggled to his feet. "My train's leaving in an hour so I have to go. Soon as I quit hobbling around I'm going back. Me and General MacArthur aim to return." Once more Sweeny smiled at the girl who had risen when he did. "Before that, though, I'm heading home to see my girl and folks."

"God bless you." Candleshine kissed his leathery cheek.

He swung out, leaning a bit on his crutch,

then made the universal V-for-Victory sign with his right hand and gallantly saluted. She watched him out of sight, the embodiment of the spirit of America, and silently prayed for his safety.

"Will you be home for Christmas?" Trinity asked on a rare visit when Candleshine had been given a little time off from her ever-increasing duties.

"No, the government has asked civilians not to travel so there will be more plane and train space for servicemen. Besides, I can do so much good with the homesick GIs who can't go home."

"We've been saving our gasoline, just in case," Will put in. He as well as Trinity showed the effects of war and worry. Silver streaks mingled with brown in his curly hair. "Suppose we come down and find a restaurant for an early holiday."

"I'd love it." Candleshine sighed. "Mom, Dad, if only I could do more! Why don't I get approval so I can go overseas?"

"When that's what God wants you to do, it will happen," Will quietly reminded her.

Her blue eyes looked almost black in her thin face. "I know, but waiting must be even worse than actually being in the middle of things."

"When you grow impatient, think of Bruce and Winona, how they must feel. And Connie."

Candleshine had never felt so selfish in her life. She was fed as well as rationing would allow at the hospital and even better at home where her parents raised almost everything. Thousands of miles away Bruce and Winona existed on scraps. She couldn't even envision the hardship that surrounded them.

Candleshine remembered the latest of the few letters she had received from Connie. Although she sounded cheerful, describing how the relocated people refused to become bitter against their country, how they ordered things from catalogs to brighten their existence, she felt the underlying mood. The worst thing about communal living was the lack of privacy. Connie and her family had taught Candleshine how important the individual family unit's privacy was to their lifestyle. How did the Imotos survive in the same quarters, with little chance to be alone? Shame erased her impatience. With so much need before her right at Mercy Hospital, longing for new pastures in which to serve was inexcusable.

The war years created a lifestyle and mood not to be duplicated again. War bonds. Rationing. Frozen jobs. Women flocked to factories by the thousands to meet the demand for planes and ships. Parachute packers, whose skill would mean life or death for those who used them, worked tirelessly. Trinity Thatcher struggled to interest children in history yet their minds flew with the planes that sometimes zoomed above isolated Cedar Ridge. Logging and farming, Will Thatcher and his family were always alert to the war news.

The year 1942 stumbled into 1943 and still the holocaust continued. Sometimes Candleshine wondered if even her faith in God could keep her going. Mercy Hospital's staff had changed drastically. Younger doctors vanished monthly, needed in the war efforts. Older doctors came out of retirement and gave their best. Candleshine's nursing class had dispersed literally to the ends of the earth. When word came that one of her own classmates had been killed while serving in Germany, the staff wept, and relentlessly went on serving.

Countless wounded men fell in love with Candleshine and the other nurses. Sally, a junior now, came to Candleshine's room one evening. "I know you aren't really my Big Sister," she said. "I mean, you're a graduate, not another student. But you're always there when I need you." Despondency marred her usually vivid face. "Candleshine — I'm glad you said I could call you that — I have a terrible problem."

"Miss Grey again?"

"No, Jim." A flood of tears erupted.

"The young man you've dated since high school."

"He's been working in a defense factory until he could gain enough weight to enlist," she whispered. "Now he wants us to get married before he goes. He's on furlough after basic training."

Candleshine felt old enough to be Sally's mother. She bit her lip to keep from crying out, "Don't!" Instead she quietly asked, "How do you feel about it?"

Sally wiped her tears with the handkerchief Candleshine offered. Her honest brown eyes held doubt. "I don't know. I love Jim and I always will. Shouldn't I do this for him? He might not come back. But if I marry, it means giving up my training. I couldn't just keep still and live a lie."

The words hung in the night air. Candleshine desperately prayed inside to know how to respond. Sally and Jim faced one of the major crossroads of their lives. How they chose to act would color their entire futures.

"Have you told Jim exactly how you feel and why?"

Sally's head drooped. "Not yet. He just mentioned it last night and wouldn't let me answer. He said I had to think about it but that he would be able to face anything in the world if I married him before he goes in the service."

"Sally, talk with him. Tell him how important your studies are to you. Your Jim may not even have considered how far-reaching the results of a war marriage can be."

Sally's muffled voice came from behind the handkerchief. "I — I don't know how to begin. I've prayed about it but somehow with all the problems in the world God must be too busy to answer right away."

"Anything that concerns you is big enough for His attention," Candleshine told her.

Sally raised her head. "It's not like he's just asking me to go away for a weekend," she said proudly. "Jim would never do that and neither would I. I told one of my girl-friends that when she bought a phony ring at the dime store. She said a girl should sacrifice something for her country. That's nuts. Our brave men are fighting so America will remain the upstanding country it is."

"You are very wise." Candleshine sighed.

"A few years ago the big question in the advice columns was, 'Should I let him kiss me goodnight on the first date?' Now this war has turned the world so upside down even nice people are shifting their values and accepting false ones!"

Sally smoothed her crumpled uniform and raised her head. "Thanks for listening. I'll see Jim as soon as I have time off." Her sensitive lips quivered. "I'm not exactly sure what's going to happen, but talking with you helped — a lot."

Later Candleshine pondered Sally's problem. Suppose she were in Sally's shoes, in love with a worthy young man, as Jim appeared to be. Would she have the strength to resist a hasty marriage and a few days together that might be all they would ever have? Would Sally, wise but deeply in love, make the right decision?

A week later Sally brought her Jim to meet Candleshine. She glowed with happiness, and something more. "Jim didn't know I couldn't finish training if we married," she said.

"It's what she's wanted since she wore rompers," the steady-faced young man said. "I guess I went haywire when I suggested getting married."

"Not haywire," said Candleshine, and she

impulsively laid her hand on the arm of the brand-new khaki sleeve that signified Jim had finished basic training.

"Take care of her, will you, Miss Thatcher? I mean, as long as you're here. Sally told me you're waiting for marching orders yourself."

"You are making a wise decision," Candleshine said. "I honestly believe that putting aside your own desires for the good of the country is for the best. Nurses are desperately needed, more now than ever before in history."

The look Jim gave Sally sent a lump to Candleshine's throat. "When I come home —" his voice underscored each word with absolute certainty. "When I come home we'll do it the right way. Church wedding, white dress, all the trimmings — not a quick ceremony in a stuffy little office."

Sally's eyes looked as if a small piece of heaven had dropped into her lap and Candleshine quietly left them alone with their deferred plans.

The experience brought Sally even closer to her mentor. Letters from Jim nearly always contained warm greetings to Candleshine. Sally bore up proudly, even when the message SHIPPING OUT, DESTINATION UNKNOWN, arrived. She studied harder, used every iota of training she had, and won the admiration of the formidable Miss Grey. Somehow the Superintendent had gotten wind of the proposed elopement and final decision and had called Sally in to congratulate her. The student nurse floated around Mercy Hospital for a good week.

"Haven't you ever been in love?" Sally blurted out one day when she and Candleshine were assigned to the same ward and met in the linen room.

"What makes you ask?" Candleshine felt more astonished than angry.

"Just about every GI you take care of is either gone or at least half-gone on you." Sally peeked out from behind a stack of precariously balanced clean sheets.

"Here, let me help." Candleshine quickly shifted the mountain. "You know these men are just homesick and missing their own girls. They fall in and out of love with all the nurses. It's our job not to take them seriously."

"How can you help it?" Sally rolled her brown eyes. "Some of the officers are so dreamy. If I didn't already have the greatest guy God ever created in the twentieth century, I'd have no will power at all!" She giggled. "I guess maybe with you it isn't will power but *won't* power. You won't let any of the guys get beyond a patient-nurse relationship."

You don't know the half of it, Candleshine thought even while she nodded. The hospital grapevine had it that Candleshine didn't even give a goodnight kiss to the few *doctors* she occasionally dated!

"Can't help it," she muttered when Sally disappeared with her sheets. "If I don't care about a man, I'm not going to let him think I do." She finished her work and shut the linen room door behind her with a little bang. "Someday, when skies smile and the world is free, I'll meet the person God already knows I will marry. Until then, forget it. Period."

The ring of a bell that signalled someone needed her drove errant thoughts away and Nurse Thatcher responded on swift and silent feet.

Five

Lieutenant Jeffrey Fairfax knelt and laid a sheaf of wild roses between the twin new mounds in the tiny western Montana cemetery. His unseeing deep blue eyes, so dark they looked black in times of emotion, barely registered the distant, snow-capped peaks and gentle breeze that relieved the dry heat. Slowly waving hemlocks and cedars forever stood sentinel over the dead.

If he had been home, would Dad and Mom still be alive?

He bared his head and the sympathetic sun sent blue shadows dancing in his black hair. He would never know. Heartsore and numb, he muttered, "What a way to come home."

A little shiver went through his six-foot muscular frame. Darkly tanned hands clasped around one knee and he remained kneeling, his head bowed.

A callused hand fell on his shoulder as a

ragged voice brought him back to life. "Jeff, boy, you couldn't have done a thing. Your daddy and mother would still have rushed to Kalispell when the call came about your aunt being sick." John Carson, foreman of the Laughing X Ranch for thirty years, shook a bent forefinger at the uniformed man then cleared his throat. "So long as there's trains, there's gonna be wrecks. Doc said your folks were killed instantly. They didn't have to suffer." Carson's hand dropped as he made circles in the earth with a dusty toed boot.

Jeff stood no taller than the white-haired foreman and no stronger, despite the difference between twenty-five and fifty-five years. Carson represented the last of the trail-hardened western breed who actually made a living running cattle and horses. By shrewdly adding new, improved methods to his wealth of knowledge, Carson's keen blue eyes could see trouble coming and handle it before it got to the ranch, *but not this time.*

"Well, boy," said Carson, shoving his battered Stetson to the back of his head, "what next?" He followed Jeff's rapid stride down from the knoll and across sage and juniper to the sprawling Fairfax ranchhouse that gleamed as white as the day the first pioneering Fairfax built it for his wife. More at home in the saddle than on foot, Carson surprisingly kept up with his pensive friend.

Once inside the comfortable house Jeff prowled the length and width of the worn but attractive living room. Polished wood floors and bright Indian blankets, harmoniously blended with good furniture and a few choice paintings, gave the room Old West charm. A rock fireplace that could accommodate a Bunyan-sized log now housed only dead ashes.

Carson's uncanny ability to understand Jeff became evident once again. "The way I see it, the good Lord did it right. Can you imagine if just one of them had been taken?"

"No," Jeff muttered softly. Their eyes met and held in wordless recognition of the unusual bond of love between Jeff's parents.

Carson's face softened. "I know it's a rotten homecomin' for you. No two folks ever had more pride than what they felt about you, boy."

Jeff squirmed, as he remembered a few best-hidden things in his life Dad and Mom never knew.

"Why, it seems like just last week when you up and said you weren't goin' to college and your daddy reckoned you were." A reminiscent light shone in the faithful foreman's eyes. "I recollect him standing right there at the corner of the fireplace, his face set hard as the rocks that made it, saying, 'You're going, Jeff. Once you're done you can come back and take over the ranch and your mother and I will give thanks and rejoice forever.' He wanted you to marry a good girl and fill this old ranchhouse with pattering feet and laughter. But first, he knew you got to know a whole lot more than even a range-trained high school boy. Learn about the rest of the world. You may think the Laughing X is the nearest place to heaven that God ever put on this earth, he used to say. But he knew once you learned what's on the other side of those mountains, you'd understand that we live in troubled times."

Carson took a deep breath and Jeff stayed nailed to the spot. He remembered that conversation as easily as Carson.

"Your dad wanted you to go out, learn what you could about life, and come back, a full partner in the Laughing X."

Carson abruptly changed the subject. "When all's been said, just remember your folks believed dyin' wasn't all that different than ridin' out of sight to new territory across the mountains."

"What do you believe?" Jeff demanded.

"*Me?*" Carson's brows rose. "I reckon

they were right." His blue gaze sharpened. "You'd better, too, what with all this fightin' you'll be in, and soon, I'd say. You'd have been in it a lot sooner if the good old U.S. didn't need our cattle so much they up and ordered you to stay home." Carson cackled. "Thought I'd never see so much letter writin' as you did to convince them you should go when the way I hear it, there are those who are writin' a passel of letters to get out of the service!"

"Dirty slackers." The little smile Jeff wore had faded. "We had them when Dad fought in World War I. Now we've got them again."

Carson sighed. "I won't say it's gonna be easy here with all our boys joinin' up." He snorted. "The bunch of pilgrims I'm able to hire these days shoulda stayed in the old folks home. I ain't complainin', though, at least not much. I aim to help win this war by raisin' the best beef in Montana so our boys can eat right." His leathered face crackled into a grin. "Just look at that." He pointed toward the open window that framed prime steers, each with the Laughing)(brand on its flank.

"Wonder how long it will take to whip our enemies so I can get back here?" Jeff mused.

Carson's satisfaction died. "I think we're in for a long, hard war, boy." He stood and stretched then froze, his hands still in the air. "Uh-oh. Here's trouble."

Jeff's sharp ears caught the whine of a car motor he'd learned to dread in the week he'd been home. "What's she doing here, anyway?" he said furiously.

"Well, she sure didn't come to see me," said Carson chuckling. "You've faced wild steers and mountain lions, coyotes and wolves. I reckon you can handle one little-bitty city gal." He hurried across the room and out the back door.

Jeffrey muttered something more descriptive than elegant and strode to the wide-roofed porch. Right now he'd take one of each of the animals Carson had mentioned rather than meet Lillian Grover!

He dispassionately surveyed the small woman whose platinum hair and delicate makeup were her trademark. A lovely face, no, a lovely *mask,* like those worn at fancy balls. Why in thunder had he ever been polite to her when introduced by a friend at college? She must be in her early thirties although she didn't look it.

Jeff sighed. Fairfax hospitality demanded at least a lukewarm reception. He walked down the steps to the graveled half-circle driveway. "Hello, Lillian, what brings you out here?"

84

"Oh, Jeff!" Suddenly the ingenue, she clapped her hands and ran to him on tiny, spiked heels. A wave of cloying perfume polluted the fresh Montana air and the rustle of silk seemed out of place against the rustic Laughing X terrain.

"I have the most wonderful news," she bubbled after Jeff seated her in a big porch chair and haughtily brought ice-cold lemonade instead of the drink she demanded. When he told her no one on the Laughing X drank — or didn't remain on the ranch if they did — Lillian didn't seem fazed at all.

"You know my father's in big with the powers that be," she reminded, as she had before on the few occasions he'd seen her. "Well, it's the same as arranged. All you have to do is sign the final papers and you have a total deferment." She beamed and her pale blue eyes wore an unusual sparkle.

"What?" Jeff sloshed his lemonade until it spilled on his pants. His eyes narrowed and the tiny wrinkles caused by the sun and hours of watching long distances increased.

"It's a surprise. I didn't say anything until Father got approval. You're to be his top advisory assistant in his plant. You know he's making munitions now instead of cars."

For the first time in his life, Jeffrey Fairfax

lost all power of speech. *How dare she interfere in his life? What right did Lillian Grover have to arrange his future? Most important, just what game did she play?* She certainly didn't think he cared about her, did she? Jeff wanted to laugh. Even if he hadn't been too busy with college to be interested in young women other than as casual dates, Lillian or any woman like her would be the last type he'd admire.

"Just what's the idea?" he asked ominously.

Lillian slowly sipped her lemonade and lowered the dark eyelashes so strangely out of place with her silvery hair. She glanced up through them with a look Jeff recognized and found unappealing. "We — I — you, Jeff." Her hands played with the small handbag in her skirted lap. "From the time we met, I felt an immediate flow between us. When you talked about the Laughing X it sounded heavenly." She turned toward the rolling reaches of the Fairfax spread and her eyes glistened.

Good heavens, this woman must think I'm rich! Knowledge struck Jeff like a lightning bolt. He quickly said, "It's nothing like heaven when northers rip and the summer sun beats down. A woman like you would freeze or shrivel out here."

Storm signals came to the pale blue eyes. "I'm tougher than I look, Jeff."

I'll just bet you are. Jeff smothered a grin.

"Besides, we — a person wouldn't have to live out here all the time. You have competent hired hands, don't you?"

Jeff almost choked. He could just see Carson if he ever heard little Miss Silk-and-Ruffles dismissing his position in that off-hand voice!

"Lillian, I hate to be inhospitable," said Jeff, deliberately glancing at the lowering sun. "But it's a long way back to the city and frankly, this isn't a good time to visit. I came home when Dad and Mom died in a train accident, and —"

"I know." Sympathy dripped from her voice. "Why, the very minute I heard the news I knew you'd be back so I canceled a dozen engagements and came as soon as I could."

Fury crept into Jeff's heart. This silly but determined woman had obviously kept track of his movements! How long had her surveillance been in effect? All through the time he remained on the ranch waiting for orders?

"I really think you'd better go." He shed his former courtesy, wondering if later he'd regret being the first Fairfax ever to dismiss a guest from the Laughing X. "Carson and I have much to discuss and I won't be home long. Thank you for taking the trouble to look up such a casual acquaintance." He stood.

If his dart found its mark, Lillian didn't let it show. She merely smiled. "Sit back down, Jeff. I'm not finished."

"Oh?" He cocked an eyebrow and again his eyes turned midnight blue. "Excuse me if I didn't say I am not interested in working in the munitions factory. I have a job to do and it will be overseas as soon as I can get things squared away here."

"Don't be stubborn. You're too important to become cannon fodder."

"I won't be facing cannons. I'll be flying. Dad and Mom encouraged me to take lessons years ago; they thought maybe someday we'd be able to have a small plane. Things didn't work out, though. We never had the money. On the other hand, now I can use my flying skills to serve my country." He looked at her curiously. "With every American desperately needed, how are *you* going to serve, Lillian? As a nurse, or maybe in the women's armed forces?"

"Heavens, no!" She shuddered. "My nerves are far too delicate for that. I'm doing a really *important* job, getting up all kinds of morale-boosting entertainment for the servicemen, recruiting attractive girls to work in the USO. Daddy's working on my getting sent to Washington, D.C." She slanted a glance at him. "That's not far from his munitions plant, you know."

"How did you ever happen to go to college in Montana?" he asked irrelevantly, wishing she'd go.

Lillian laughed. "I didn't have the grades for a big-name eastern school. Besides, Daddy wants to get into politics and being a big toad in a small state like Montana could be a first step. He thought my attending school out here would give him some good publicity, you know, 'Daughter of important Montana-born millionaire chooses home state' kind of thing."

With an eellike movement, she slipped from her chair and stood next to him. "That uniform looks good on you, Jeff. Too bad you won't be wearing it at the plant. Or —" She considered for a moment. "I could have Daddy do some wangling and get you a Washington assignment. It's too bad for you to have to go back in civvies."

"I won't be." He smiled as he thought of sending her flying down the steps, out of sight and back where she belonged. "Thanks again for coming, but I have work to do."

Lillian's pretty face turned mutinous.

"Carson?" Jeff called.

The lively foreman appeared faster than you could say Laughing X Ranch. "Right here."

"Miss Grover's ready to go now so we can get back to our ways and means committee of two. I'll be in by the time you get a pot of coffee going. We'll delay supper for a time and get at our problems."

"Drive carefully," Carson told Lillian before disappearing into the ranchhouse.

Jeffrey piloted her to her expensive car, talking all the way to stop the protest he knew trembled on her painted lips. He ended with a firm handshake. "I know you're busy and so am I so I'll just say goodbye now. If you see any of the college crowd, give them my greetings. Maybe someday after this war ends we can have a reunion."

Silenced by a determination that overshadowed her own, Lillian angrily jerked her car into gear and shot out of the driveway after calling, "I'll be in touch about the post in Washington!"

"Good riddance." Jeff stalked up the steps, across the porch, and inside the sprawling home.

"Reminds me of a filly that needs to be

broke," Carson reflected. "Pretty as paint but too much paint to suit me." He glanced at the large, framed photograph of Jeff's parents that hung over the mantel. An unaccustomed mist clouded his old blue eyes and Jeff saw his hands clench and then relax. "Boy, if ever you bring home a gal, get one like your mother."

"I will. . . ." Jeff's voice trailed off and the work he'd called pressing seemed to dim. "Are there any more like her? I'm old-fashioned, I guess, but I can't stomach women like Lillian Grover — and since this blamed war started, I'm seeing a lot of them!"

"She shoulda been turned over her pa's knee when she was small."

"How come you never slipped into a double harness?" Jeff asked Carson.

"I'm a one-woman man and besides she married someone else," Carson said quietly, causing Jeff to regret the question.

That woman was Mom, Jeff suddenly knew, but he didn't let on. Carson's well-hidden secret would remain his own unless he chose to tell it.

Instead, Carson turned from the photograph to Jeff and said, "Let's get down to facts and figures."

As much as Jeff loved the Laughing X, demands and all, he chafed under the necessary restrictions that kept him in Montana and not on his way overseas. He agreed with Carson that everything must be left in the best possible condition to raise the best beef in Montana for the troops. Dawn to dusk Jeff, Carson, and the hands Carson called pilgrims rode hills and valleys, rounded up strays, and counted cattle and horses.

"I don't hire aliens," Jeff curtly told three men one afternoon. "If a man's not willing to take out citizenship papers, then there's no place for him here."

Carson's eyes flashed. "You didn't have to tell me that."

"I know." Jeff's steady gaze simmered down his irascible foreman. "You can run this place with both hands tied and one foot missing. At least I don't have that to worry about." His brows knitted into a clean, black line. "Wish I could say the same about other things."

"Such as how to duck outa sight when Miss Grover shows?" Carson's teeth gleamed in a wolfish smile. "Say, want me to get rid of her for you?"

"Yeah, if you can without nailing her hide to the barn door."

Carson's eyes beamed with satisfaction. "Next time that little ol' auto of hers comes bouncin' in, leave it to me. But if you want to have some fun, stick close enough to hear."

A few days later Carson got his chance. Puffs of dust on the valley road heralded Lillian's approach. This time instead of flinging himself on a bare-backed horse, Jeff crouched just inside the big casement window off the front porch, fervently praying Lillian wouldn't suddenly find a reason to come inside.

"Where's Jeff, Carson?" Lillian's crisp voice little resembled the tone she used for her quarry.

"I saw him ride off earlier," Carson said truthfully and failed to add he'd also seen him return. "Miss Grover, may I be so bold as to get your advice, about Jeff, I mean?"

"Why, of course." She came up the steps and sat down while Jeff stuffed his fist in his mouth to keep from betraying his presence.

"It's like this. A long time ago the Laughing X made money. Then came the Depression and now with the war —"

Jeff couldn't resist raising his head and peeking through the window to where Carson sat on the porch rail facing Lillian and the house, his face bland and eyes innocent.

"You mean it's not a paying proposition

any more?" The small woman's incisive voice cut through Carson's hesitation.

"Let's just say we're not sellin' beef the way we used to."

Jeff was in agony. Wily Carson, who scorned to tell a lie but only told part of the truth. Of course they weren't selling beef just now, and wouldn't until roundup a few weeks off!

"I was wonderin', your daddy's got a lot of money and all. Think he'd be willin' to give Jeff a helpin' hand?"

A cold chill slid down Jeff's spine. Had Carson overplayed his little scene? He felt sure of it when Lillian spoke.

"He'd help but only to get Jeff in his factory or behind a desk in Washington, Carson. I don't plan to marry a rancher, especially if he's running a downhill place."

"Marry?" Carson's hand stroking his unshaven chin sounded like a buzz saw. "You're right, Miss Grover. A rancher's the worst kind of man to tie to, 'specially one like Jeff. Why, he'd expect you to come right out here and take charge of the house. Our cook's been mutterin' about askin' for his time — say, can you cook and clean and milk cows?"

Lillian's gasp reached Jeff's ears. She hastily rose. "Carson, I want a straight answer. How tied to the Laughing X is Jeff? I'm getting discouraged trying to get him to agree to leave it."

Carson stood and swept off his stained Stetson. His poignant blue eyes shone like mountain lakes. "Miss Grover, this place, such as it is, why, it's Jeff's *life.* Never under God's blue sky will Jeffrey Fairfax live anywhere else. Now if you're willin' to accept that and come make a home for him —"

"Never." She exhaled loudly before running down the steps.

Heedless of giving himself away, Jeff peered out the window and saw the defeat in Lillian's face.

"I'd just as soon you didn't mention our little talk to Jeff." She saucily blew Carson a kiss. "Thanks for letting me know how things are. Oh, tell Jeff I've gone to Washington. Daddy's been wanting me to come back." Her racy car left dust whirls as she fled from the idea of ranch life.

"I think I'll give you a raise," Jeff said stepping onto the porch. Their laughter rang across the ranch and Carson slowly nodded.

A week later Jeff's orders came for overseas duty.

Six

Miss Grey shuffled papers in front of her and let her hands rest on them. The same clear, gray gaze that had once terrified Candleshine now looked deeply into her top nurse's sparkling eyes. "You'll be leaving us soon. Your orders have come through. Your country needs you even more than we here at Mercy Hospital, if that's possible." A little sigh escaped the Superintendent's lips.

How tired and old she looks, Candleshine thought before she said, "I'm glad the waiting is over."

"Someday, when this insanity is over, you'll come back to us?" Miss Grey's voice actually trembled and concern spilled into the room.

"If I can, or if Bruce doesn't need me elsewhere."

A hundred feelings rose within her: relief; sadness at leaving the hospital and Hunter Hall, her home for years; excitement and fear of the future; inadequacy. Would everything she had learned here, the hundreds of hours of training and ward work, be enough to sustain her and save lives?

"Miss Grey, am I ready?" Her impulsive question burst out like a grenade.

Her supervisor's head shot up. Her eyes steeled and once more she became the dreadnaught of Candleshine's early training days. "Of course you're ready, Miss Thatcher!" She rose in the magnificent motion that signalled the end of the interview. "No nurse trained by Mercy Hospital and kept on afterward will fail in duty, *whatever that duty may be*."

Candleshine relaxed and let an impish grin curl her lips upward as she stood and started for the door.

"Here are your orders. You'll be transported on the troop ship *Fortitude*." Miss Grey swept the papers into a bunch and handed them over.

Candleshine barely glanced at them but she caught one word. "Australia?"

"Your skills will be desperately in demand. The nurses there have performed magnificently but human flesh can only carry on so long." All pretense between them fell for a telling moment. "Candleshine, child, go with God's blessing, and mine."

The younger nurse swallowed hard. "Th— thank you, Miss Grey. I'll try to be a credit to Mercy Hospital." *And to you,* she mentally added, knowing by the softness in Miss Grey's eyes those unspoken words came through clearly.

Candleshine felt she had left part of herself behind when she finally stowed the last of her possessions in the family car and Will headed for Cedar Ridge. "I'm glad for the days I have in between," she quietly said. "It's like changing from one life to another. Home is the neutral zone, my security."

Trinity clenched her hands tight in her lap and nodded. Will's hands tightened on the steering wheel.

"Mom, Dad, I'm going to be all right," Candleshine continued. "You know for years I've felt God wanted me to go. You've taught me He will be there with me the same way He went with me to training school."

Will cleared his throat. "It's a mite farther to Australia than to Seattle, honey. Like you said, though, God's everywhere." He took a deep breath. "Wait 'til you see what Trinity's done to the house since you were home last."

Successfully sidetracked, Candleshine turned toward her mother. "What this time?" She smiled, remembering childhood days when one of "Mom's decorating spells" left their house in confusion for days and ended with newly papered walls or fresh paint on cupboards and furniture.

"You'll see soon enough." Trinity smiled mysteriously.

A few hours later the ecstatic girl viewed her redecorated bedroom. White walls and ceilings brightened and lightened the big, square room. Chintz curtains with sprigs of lilacs matched the bedspread. New lilac dressing table appointments tied the room together and a leaf-green floor covering gave the feeling of being in the middle of a Cedar Ridge spring.

"It's gorgeous," she cried. "I suppose you made the long curtains?"

"Of course. Yardage is less expensive than finished curtains. Besides, I wanted to add a few extra touches." Trinity fingered the crisp material.

"Was any girl ever luckier or more blessed with better parents?" Candleshine dropped to the soft bed and let its familiar contours erase the tension that had built ever since her long-awaited orders came.

"We think we were pretty lucky *and* blessed to have such a daughter," Will observed from the doorway where he lounged against the jamb.

"You'll write, won't you?" The full meaning of thousands of miles of looming ocean rose in the young nurse's mind.

"Haven't we always?" her father demanded in mock indignation.

"Where do you get the *we?*" Candleshine teased. "Mom writes and writes. I'm lucky to get a postscript from you."

Will's round blue eyes took on a look of aggrieved innocence. "Now, what's the use of my repeating all the news your mother already has said?"

"You fraud!" She sent him a smile that said more loudly than words that she saw through him and loved him because of it.

Candleshine hadn't known how much she needed her neutral zone. The first few days passed in a blur of memories. She knew the time just before leaving would be one of looking ahead. The precious middle days would restore her sorely tried strength and peace of mind and free her from past turmoil. She walked, visited relatives and friends, and rode horseback. She climbed and ate like a harvest hand. She slept in the still, black, untroubled nights better than she had done in years, clinging to her oasis in the middle of the world's shifting sands.

There had been no news of Bruce or Winona. A few straggly letters from Connie continued to speak of the incredible way those in the relocation camp kept up morale and waited. How far away it seemed from their struggling training days! A letter from Sally Monroe allowed Candleshine a glimpse into the younger girl's heart. "If I can ever be half the nurse you are, I will have fulfilled God's calling to me," Sally wrote. "Now that you're gone, I'm trying to be to some of the beginning students what you were, rather *are,* to me." Sally finished on a touching note. "I'm holding the torch high, Candleshine." Below the signature Sally added, "P.S. I hope the war is over before I graduate. If it isn't, I'm joining up with either the army or navy and help win it myself!"

"She'll do it, too," Candleshine told her folks, her eyes shining. "That girl has the ability to be one of the greatest nurses ever. Her heart and head and hands work in perfect balance."

The next day she wrote back to her self-appointed protégée. "Whatever field of nursing you choose will be fortunate to have you, Sally. I am a better person because of your faith in me." She licked the envelope then hastily reopened it and scribbled on the bottom of her letter, "Take care of Miss Grey, if you can. She bears such a heavy load. She won't accept sympathy or much outward friendship but just doing your work plus a little more and encouraging others to do the same can make a real difference." Relieved by the knowledge Sally would follow instructions to the letter, as she had in her training and ward work, Candleshine quickly stamped the envelope and raced to the mail box so the rural carrier would pick it up on her rounds.

Years earlier Candleshine had found the buildings in Seattle enormous to her rural eyes. When she and other nurses boarded the *Fortitude* she felt much the same way. The troop ship that carried hundreds of persons, food, medicine, and supplies to keep it self-sustaining was in many ways a floating city! It didn't take long for her to recognize the determination of everyone aboard. Most of the nurses had already seen battle but not one of the older women made Candleshine feel unwelcome or without value. Rather, they greeted her with enthusiasm and warmth. Every pair of trained hands meant relief to the wounded and respite to the overworked nurses in Australia.

Before the *Fortitude* ever reached its destination, Candleshine found her skills in demand. She proved to be a surprisingly good sailor, even when a storm the ship's commander identified as "just this side of a typhoon" tossed the staunch troop ship high one moment and sucked it deep between waves the next. The crowded quarters didn't help either. Candleshine did all she could to relieve those of her cabin mates who succumbed to seasickness then volunteered to the ship's doctor and spent long hours working with those in sick bay.

One husky soldier eyed her suspiciously. "How come a gal like you trots around brighter than a July day and us poor slobs that're s'posed to be the stronger sex wind up being the patients?"

"I honestly don't know," she confessed. The young nurse's candor brought a laugh from everyone who heard and many passed on the remark.

Other than in her official duties, Candleshine had little contact with the troops. The nurses' quarters remained off-limits. Even when she went topside after the storms abated, the men respectfully kept their distance except to smile, nod, or give a brief greeting.

The crossing of the equator changed everything.

"Wait 'til you see the initiation," one of the veteran nurses told Candleshine.

"Initiation? For what?"

The older woman's eyes twinkled. "For the troops who are crossing the equator for the first time. We'll keep back out of sight but you don't want to miss it."

Something in her voice put Candleshine on alert. When the crossing time came she hid herself in a well-screened corner and stuffed her hands in her mouth as raw eggs squashed on unsuspecting heads in the traditional equator initiation. Someday, when her letters would not fall under the censor's stamp due to possible detection of the *Fortitude* and its movements, she would write home. How Dad would howl at this grotesque comedy in the middle of a war!

The stories that floated around the ship had begun to make Candleshine feel at home. While she expertly wrapped a staff sergeant's sprained ankle after a doctor's examination, there was this exchange.

"Hey, Nurse Thatcher, I must be living right."

"I hope so," she told him and kept on wrapping.

"No, really." His sunburned face lit up like a Cedar Ridge full moon. "I got wise to the initiation and ducked out." He grimaced as her gentle fingers touched a tender spot.

"Really? I thought everyone had to participate." She eyed him suspiciously.

"Oh, I got three days of latrine duty for not showing," he admitted. "That's the best part of the whole thing."

"First time I've heard that latrine duty's so welcome." Candleshine's blue eyes snapped with fun.

The staff sergeant dropped his joking. "It gave me a chance to talk tactics with some second lieutenants just out of officer candidate school." His keen gaze penetrated her doubts. "The more I know about such things, the better I can do my own job. Those second lieutenants are a whole lot smarter than some give them credit for. You watch and see — the so-called ninety-day wonders will turn out okay in spite of what some of the noncoms think."

Time crawled by. One night Candleshine slipped topside, feeling crowded by her small, shared quarters. Even in Hunter Hall she had been in a single room. Learning to live day after uncertain day surrounded by people at all times left her longing for freedom. She knew the necessary peace she required lay over the *Fortitude's* rail. The Pacific Ocean in its newly settled state offered wide vistas to relax tired eyes and spirits.

She sank on a pile of rope neatly coiled and closed her eyes for a moment as she whispered a prayer. When she opened her eyes again, she gasped. Never in all the days at Cedar Ridge had she seen such a gorgeous sight.

The clear night spread an inverted bowl above her. Dark blue velvet canopied the sky and hosted stars that looked close enough to gather. Yet even their grandeur faded when she turned her head a bit to one side.

The Southern Cross constellation she had read of in geography books hung above her as if suspended on a string. Its perfect crossbar of space shimmered in the heavens, a symbol of hope to the weary even as the cross of Calvary offered hope and salvation. The four glittering stars lighting the southern hemisphere were steady and sublime, never to be forgotten by any who saw with hearts as well as eyes.

Candleshine felt warm drops slide onto her clasped hands. Oh, that she were a poet to describe the night! Who could see such indescribable beauty and deny the existence of a Creator?

When I consider thy heavens, the work of thy fingers, the moon and the stars, which thou hast ordained; What is man, that thou art mindful of him? and the son of man, that thou visiteth him?*

*Psalm 8:3,4 (KJV).

Candleshine trembled. Had someone spoken? No, the night remained still, the ocean in surrender. The memory verse she had learned years before echoed in her heart. Drawn closer to her Heavenly Father by the night glory, at last she reluctantly left her post and slipped below deck. Yet the glowing Southern Cross remained with her and the feeling she had seen the hand of God.

The first time Candleshine heard firing in the distance and saw the sky torn apart and aglow with wicked light, it took all her ancestral courage to keep from hiding in her bunk. Closer and closer they drew to the actual fighting, sliding through the dangerous waters like an avenging angel. Nerves were pitched to the breaking point. News grew nonexistent with the need for increased security, and even most of the scuttlebutt died.

The air attacks intensified. How could the *Fortitude* escape? Candleshine hid her fear and continued caring for those who needed her, praying continuously.

One black night she awoke when a violent jolt threw her from her bunk. Incredibly she had learned to sleep in the middle of noise and tumult. The cries from her cabin mates, the warning gong of the ship's bell that signalled all hands to deck, and the chilling words, "We're hit" brought her scrambling into her clothes as best she could. Minutes later the deserted cabin held a welter of discarded clothes. Each nurse had grabbed her medical bag and the single already-packed bag of necessities and hurried topside.

Even as the Southern Cross defied description, so did the scene of horror that awaited them. Candleshine felt chilled to the bone despite the heat from flames on the starboard side of the ship. "Big trouble," a black-faced, half-dressed soldier called. His teeth bared, he reassured the nurses. "We aren't sinking or anything like that. But just in case that Zero comes back, get your lifejackets on."

Would she awake to find this only one more nightmare? Candleshine wondered. She pinched herself, hard. This was no dream but the real thing.

"Is anyone hurt?" an older nurse demanded.

"Yeah. Over there."

"Come on, no time to loiter now." The speaker took command. "Thatcher, move it."

The order freed Candleshine. She obediently ran after the others. After what seemed an eternity of caring for burned and bleeding men, word came to the crew and nurses the fire had been stopped. Unfortunately, one of the engines had been affected. The *Fortitude* could continue sailing but a turgid flow of oil was staining the ocean waters.

The ship's commander ordered everyone on deck. "We're going to change course. We'll never make it to our original destination. We're in no danger at the present time." His sardonic face broke into a sour smile. "At least no more than we have been. We do have to get somewhere and lay over for repairs, though. Keep ready. There's no written-in-blood guarantee we won't take another hit."

Candleshine barely heard him. Now that the immediate danger had lessened, a multitude of men who had shrugged off burns and wounds as nothing to fight the fire needed her attention.

"Where will we go?" In consternation she looked at the same staff sergeant she'd cared for earlier. "I'm sorry. I know I shouldn't have asked that."

His massive, sweaty shoulders shrugged and he didn't even flinch when she dressed an angry red burn that ran from shoulder to wrist. In a low voice he told her, "Keep it under your hat and I may be wrong but I'd guess we'll head for Guadalcanal in the Solomons. The Japanese evacuated it in February after a vicious six-month battle. Admiral Halsey's working his way up the islands." He grinned at her. "Of course, I could be wrong. I have been once or twice."

"At least you admit it." Candleshine smiled back.

"Say, if we get parked on Guadalcanal for repairs you'll see something. It's 2500 square miles, has a 7000- or 8000-foot mountain range in the middle, and a sharp drop to the sea on one side, a gentle one on the other. Coconuts, pineapples, bananas, and tropical forests, they're all there. The Japanese were building an air base so they could attack our ships but we surprised them."

"You're better than a tour guide," Candleshine told him.

"Listen, when I knew I might get sent somewhere out here I made sure I got some smarts about things." His grim voice made her feel ashamed for twitting him but his ready smile flashed again. "The Melanesians — they're the dark-skinned people who live on Guadal — build their houses on stilts. Keeps them cooler. If things were different it'd be one great place for a vacation. Temperatures between 70 and 90 degrees all the time and lots of rain to keep things green. 'Course I don't know how much greenery's left after the fighting. It may be pretty bleak."

"How long do you think it will take to get the *Fortitude* patched up?" Candleshine couldn't resist asking. She snipped off the end of the gauze with her curved bandage scissors and tucked it in.

Her friendly informant grunted. "No way to tell. What's the matter? Don't you want a Guadalcanal vacation?" His teasing smile put things back in proportion.

The *Fortitude* limped toward Guadalcanal, leaving behind unerasable oily evidence. The few times Candleshine chanced to see the ship's commander, he appeared a decade older and his stern face sent shivers through her. She felt without asking that he feared another attack that would make arrival on Guadalcanal impossible. The nurses slept lightly, ever on the alert for the inevitable.

Like a swarm of angry bees Japanese fighter pilots discovered and attacked the *Fortitude*, miraculously avoiding the answering antiaircraft that had begun firing immediately when the fighter planes appeared. Yet the boom of the ship's cannon and the belching shells from the long-barrelled antiaircraft guns sent the enemies on their way.

Hope of reaching Guadalcanal died an instant death. In a subdued but undefeated voice, the commanding officer ordered the evacuation of the Fortitude. As the survivors of the night attack huddled in lifeboats and wondered what lay ahead, only the moans of the badly wounded mingled with the ocean's roar in an eerie duet.

Seven

For three days the lifeboats from the sunken *Fortitude* battled a malicious storm determined to defeat them. Candleshine and the one other nurse on her lifeboat did all they could to help the wounded. A hundred times Miss Grey's crisp statement, *No nurse trained by Mercy Hospital will fail in duty, whatever that duty may be,* bolstered Candleshine's sagging spirits. She set her lips and went on, hampered by lack of shelter against the beating rain and lack of proper space to allow those in the boat to lie down and rest.

Twice during those three days Japanese fighter planes appeared in the leaden skies, once in the distance and once swooping toward them only to be intercepted by Allied planes that drove them away. Too numb from fear and exposure to care, Candleshine continued cleansing wounds, wiping sweaty faces, and whispering encouragement.

Once when her charges restlessly tossed with the never-ending motion of the waves she hummed an old hymn. An uneasy peace settled over her patients.

"Sing the words," a soldier still in his teens asked through fever-parched lips, his eyes blinking back drops.

Candleshine dampened a handkerchief and wiped his face again as she sang, " 'Jesus is calling! O hear him today, Calling for you, Calling for you.' " When she came to the chorus one bass voice joined in, then another.

Calling for you; Calling for you!
Hear him today; do not turn him away!
Jesus is calling for you.

Even the sullen storm could not withstand the surge of renewed hope that swept over the little group. The only other lifeboat that had remained in sight through the driving rain echoed back the song.

Jesus is calling! He stands at the door. . . .

Suddenly Candleshine could sing no longer. These gallant comrades were defying the forces of nature in unfamiliar waters with the immortal words of a hymn many had learned at their mothers' knees. Nothing so far threatened to shake her as this had done.

"More," someone pleaded.

Until voices grew so hoarse they could no longer utter the words, the castaways drifted from song to song and ended with "Amazing Grace." On the third stanza all the hidden fear and homesickness spilled out.

Through many dangers, toils, and snares
I have already come;
'Tis grace has brought me safe thus far,
And grace will lead me home.

No one could go on with the last verse. The word *home* conjured up scenes too powerful to deny.

A feverish hand clutched Candleshine's. "Nurse, are we going to die?"

"I don't know." Candleshine silently called on God for strength and wisdom. This young soldier, so badly hurt, needed far more than she could give on her own.

"Are you afraid?"

"Horribly." She knew every pair of ears had tuned in to the conversation. "I want to live and serve and go back home to my family." She took a deep and ragged breath then laid her free hand on the seeking one. "But if God doesn't choose to spare me, I know I will live forever in a wonderful world where war and dying and hatred can never live. I know my God cared so much for me and you and everyone that He sent His Son to die so we might live."

"I've done some pretty bad things," the soldier continued averting his gaze and nervously plucking at his uniform.

"Christ didn't come to save those who are righteous. He came to save sinners, and that means all of us."

"I used to know Him."

"He has always known and loved you." She smiled into the worried face. "Do you know the story of the lost sheep?"*

"I did when I was a kid."

Totally oblivious to the others and caught up in her desire to help this one soldier, Candleshine's voice lowered. The rain slackened and a watery shaft of light hovered.

"Jesus told a parable of a shepherd who had a hundred sheep. One got lost, we don't know how. Perhaps it strayed from the flock looking for at tempting place to graze. Maybe

*From Luke 15.

it got caught in a thorn bush. Anyway, the shepherd left the ninety-nine safely penned up and went out to find his lost sheep. He may have faced storms or danger, black nights or rough trails. The important thing is that he didn't stop searching until he found his lost sheep. He carried it home on his shoulders and called his friends and neighbors and told them to rejoice with him.

"Jesus went on to say that there is more joy in heaven over one sinner that repents than over ninety-nine just persons."

Silence greeted the story, broken by the young soldier's whispered thanks.

"Look!" Candleshine's gaze followed the pointing finger. Off to their left lay a small island.

With renewed strength, men whose blistered fingers had attempted to guide the lifeboat through the storm grabbed oars. After a guarded call to the second lifeboat, the two craft headed for shore.

"Will it be occupied?" Candleshine whispered to the other nurse.

"Who knows?" Her face set in grim lines. "We don't have much choice. Even if it is, we can't stay out here any longer. One more bad storm or another attack and. . . ."

Candleshine could guess the rest.

Slowly and cautiously the lifeboats approached the small island. Its tropical foliage could hide enemy forces. Candleshine saw coconuts and bananas and thought of the staff sergeant who had given her information on the Solomon Islands and Guadalcanal. Had he escaped death on the *Fortitude*? This island couldn't be Guadalcanal or one of the Solomons, they hadn't been that close.

"Not a sound," one of the rowers whispered. His haggard, unshaven face and taut shoulders showed his tension. *"What's that?"*

Candleshine quickly turned to the narrow coast. Her cry of joy joined the growing excitement and relief that filled the lifeboat. American soldiers stood on shore hauling three beached lifeboats out of the water. Under the cover of heavy vegetation that came almost down to the ocean, her staff sergeant was in the lead.

"Thank God! We have it to ourselves, at least for now." A few mighty strokes of the oars brought their boat into shallow water.

"Everyone out and fast," someone yelled from shore. "The Japanese have been flying low. They haven't spotted us but they act like they're suspicious."

Before he finished speaking the distant

drone of unseen planes assaulted Candle-shine's ears. She leaped into the waist-deep water, ordered those who could walk to help those who couldn't, and before the fighter planes came into sight the entire company of early arrivals and newcomers had managed to put themselves and the lifeboats out of sight. The staff sergeant and several others had even whacked off giant branches and swept clean from the sand evidence of the landing.

They crouched beneath the flimsy but interwoven green protection while the planes circled, flew away, turned, and came back again and again. From her uncomfortable position on the ground Candleshine didn't dare look up. She kept her face buried in her folded arms, wondering why the fighter pilots didn't hear the loud pounding of her heart.

Much later the staff sergeant gathered his little band. "Anyone here of higher rank than I am?" he demanded.

"Second lieutenant here," a wounded man said. He tried to sit up and fell back, his face contorted. "I'm in no condition to command."

"Anyone else?" No one answered. "Okay, if our second lieutenant can't take charge, I guess I'm it. My name's Magee and I don't want any guff about it." His eyes bored into the bedraggled crew. "The way I see it, we have to hole up here until we can make contact and be evacuated." His grimy hands nested on his wrinkled, stained khaki pants. "We hope it may be soon, but it may be later, a lot later." His far-seeing eyes scanned the horizon. "At that, we're a lot luckier than the rest of the *Fortitude* crew."

Candleshine thought of the small number on the island compared with all those who had been on the doomed ship.

"We've got rations and lots of fruit," he said, pausing to grin at Candleshine. "Coconuts and bananas and pineapples. The ocean's full of fish. We won't starve. But it's going to take every one of us working together to stay out of sight of the Japanese during our little vacation here."

His grin soon faded. "First thing we have to do is rig up a place so our nurses can take care of the wounded. Did we luck out and wind up with a doctor? No? Too bad, but we've got one, two, three nurses."

"I know some first aid," one soldier volunteered.

"Same here," another put in.

Magee stared at the two. "Your job's to do whatever you're told, okay?" He didn't wait for an answer. "The rest of you will do whatever's needed, the same as me — dig latrines, find clean water for drinking, put up some kind of shelter against the rain, collect food, and stand guard. How many weapons in the bunch?"

A show of hardware brought a pleased grunt. "We can use the tallest trees for lookout posts. Oh, there ain't anyone else on this island. Looks like the natives fled when things got hot. So we have it all nice and cozy to ourselves."

Before night willing hands had erected a rude, thatched shelter that Magee tagged "No-Name Island Hospital." The dozen or more wounded soldiers lay on hastily constructed pallets formed by piling leafy branches on the ground covered with blankets from the lifeboats. To Candleshine and her fellow nurses' delight, only the young soldier and the second lieutenant had serious wounds. If the rest could avoid tropical disease they'd be at least temporarily all right.

Staff Sergeant Magee triumphantly produced bolts of mosquito netting from the lifeboats' lockers and soon every sleeping place and the crude kitchen stood draped with netting. Mosquitoes and other insects beat against it furiously but to no avail.

"We need to set up a schedule as long as

we have critically ill patients," said Elizabeth, the older nurse from Candleshine's lifeboat who automatically took charge. "Any preference?"

The third nurse who said her name was Jane confessed, "I hated night duty every time I had it. I just can't keep awake."

"I'll take it," Candleshine volunteered.

Elizabeth's face lost some of its grimness. "Why don't we do it like this? Jane can have 6 a.m. to 2 p.m., I'll take 2 to 10 p.m. and you'll work 10 to 6, at least for now. Later when our criticals get better we'll see about time off. Those two soldiers who know first aid will spell us."

The strangest period of Candleshine's nursing career thus far began at ten that night. Candleshine had managed to nap in the hot afternoon, thankful for the "quarters" the men eagerly made for them with available materials. At first the unfamiliar bed of branches kept her awake but her ward training and the breathing exercises she knew relaxed her body. Refreshed, she began her first shift at No-Name Hospital.

What would Bruce and her family think if they could see her now, separated from the night by only a thin mosquito netting? For the first time in days she had time to think. Fragments filled her mind, keeping her awake and alert. Would she ever forget the way her brave companions sang in the lifeboats? Or how eagerly the young soldier's eyes turned to her when she recounted the story of the lost sheep?

Never! Every experience she faced must become part of her and help her hold high that torch from generations who had gone before fighting for freedom.

Candleshine smiled. Little had she known when she began nurses' training her torch would actually be a flashlight! Dimmed with a handkerchief, she had just enough light to keep an eagle eye on patients in the makeshift hospital.

A little after midnight the mosquito netting swayed and Staff Sergeant Magee stepped in. He stood with hands on hips, a now-familiar posture, then walked between the two rows of sleeping men, his step far lighter than Candleshine would have expected.

"Everything all right?" he whispered.

"Yes." She touched his arm and they stepped outside so her low voice wouldn't disturb the patients. "We have a problem in caring for the men because they're so close to the ground. It means kneeling every time we give aid. Can you and the others make some kind of cots?"

"No problem." Magee cocked his head and glanced at the surrounding foliage. Bamboo stems as thick as his wrist showed in the pale moonlight. "You know the health of our whole company depends on you three nurses. Anything you want that I can get for you, just holler and it's yours."

"Thank you, Sergeant Magee."

A slight sound behind her sent Candleshine back through the mosquito netting. The young soldier needed a drink of water, and someone to talk with.

"I've been thinking about what you said," he whispered after downing the water.

The smile that had won patients' and doctors' hearts alike back in Mercy Hospital encouraged the boy. "It's worth thinking about."

"I told Him I wished I'd stayed straight instead of going my own way," the boy said, his face flushed. "I never did anything really terrible but Mom wouldn't like knowing some things. When I get well I'm going to start telling other people how important God is." He stirred restlessly. "I'm not just saying it because I'm down and out either. I really mean it, nurse."

"I believe you." Her low voice brought a new flush to his cheeks but this time one of pleasure.

"Goodnight, soldier." She patted his hand and smiled again.

"Goodnight, nurse." He closed his eyes. A few moments later his steady breathing showed that he slept untroubled by what tomorrow might bring.

"How do you keep your faith so strong?"

Candleshine whipped around at the whisper. The second lieutenant lay prone and stared at her with unreadable eyes.

She glanced the length of her little domain, saw that all was well, and knelt beside the speaker. "As far back as I can remember I knew God was my best friend and that He cared about me." For a moment she saw herself as the small girl who confidently trotted into the presence of God eagerly spilling her childish prayers. *Please, God, make my kitty get well . . . Please, God, help me be a good girl.* Memories stung her eyelids.

"You've done a fine thing for that boy," the lieutenant said, as he nodded toward the sleeping soldier. "Is he going to make it?"

"He is if there's anything I can do about it."

"I suppose that includes praying."

Candleshine heard the wistfulness behind the statement and responded to it with her whole heart. "Lieutenant, if I didn't add prayer to the care I give, I wouldn't be giving my best."

A strong hand gripped her wrist. "You might add a second lieutenant to your list."

"I will." Her face shone in the moonlight that sneaked through the mosquito netting.

"Thanks. Goodnight, nurse." He turned to one side. She felt the tremor of his body from the slight effort. It would take the skill of all three nurses plus mighty prayer to pull him through. She smoothed his hair from his hot forehead, whispered, "Goodnight," and went back to her lonely vigil.

Uneasy hours passed, broken only by a few snores or someone asking for water. Candleshine faithfully made her rounds, as she had under far different circumstances a hundred times. Tonight Connie and Bruce and Winona seemed very close, closer than they had in weeks. Was it because she practiced her skills under primitive conditions and knew they did the same?

"God, help us all," she prayed in a quiet moment.

In the darkest hour after the moon had set and before the day began, Candleshine found herself fighting sleep. Every man in her care lay sleeping. She paced the short length of aisle between the pallets, checking and rechecking, especially her two criticals.

From training days she knew the human body sank to its lowest ebb at this time period. Patient after patient failed to pass the test and too often even those who appeared to be on the mend slipped away in the early morning hours. It was then that Candleshine prayed the hardest: for those whose lives hung on the care they received; for friends and family; for all the Sally Monroes and Miss Greys who even at this moment might also be keeping watch by night.

A fuller understanding of what it meant to be a nurse slowly came to her. Crumpled by kneeling, sustained by prayer, Candleshine experienced the humility known by all who serve their Master. When Jane came in at six to relieve her, she found Candleshine smiling with a look in her eyes never to be forgotten.

"They're all well so far. Our two criticals got some sleep and their temperatures are down," Candleshine exulted. She squared her shoulders and rubbed her neck. "All that kneeling gets to you but Sergeant Magee's going to see what he can do about it."

"Good." Jane, a few years older, beamed at her. "Anything special I need to know?"

"Just that all is well."

"That's the only thing that really matters," Jane said softly. "If I can help save someone, the way I wish my young brother could have been saved, it's all I ask."

Candleshine's quick sympathy rose as she wordlessly squeezed Jane's arm. Then Jane's clear voice rang out. "All right, men, up and at 'em. We've got faces and hands to wash before breakfast!"

A few days later Candleshine discovered Elizabeth also served because of loss, her husband, in the early days of Manila. Elizabeth expressed much the same sentiments as Jane. "I couldn't live with myself if I didn't do what I could to help win this war. It's what Tom would expect of me." The next moment her usual brusque self returned, wasting little time in what couldn't be changed when so much needed to be done now.

Thanks to Sergeant Magee, two neat lines of bamboo cots with tautly stretched thatch and blankets soon replaced the ground-level pallets. Candleshine rejoiced when she arrived for night duty and found that Elizabeth had dismissed two soldiers to regular quarters. Another proudly boasted, "A couple more days and I'll be good as new," when he hobbled back from the closest latrine on a freshly made crutch. "Hey, we musta had a visit from Santa Claus!"

Candleshine eyed the enormous stalks of bananas Sergeant Magee had thoughtfully ordered delivered to the ward. "Help yourself. There's a lot of energy in a banana." She peeled one and ate it, although supper had been filling.

Morale raised every day. Outside of one new patient who had cut his foot on sharp coral while fishing, the camp remained healthy. Sergeant Magee announced he had men working to rig up some kind of communication with the rest of the world and, in the meantime, everyone was to "eat all they could, sleep all they could, and in general, take it easy 'cause who knew where'd they go from here."

Yet the threat of detection kept Candleshine and the others from following orders to the letter. Again and again Japanese fighter planes hovered above No-Name Island while its inhabitants froze beneath their camouflage and waited for the sound of bombs that must inevitably come.

Eight

Nothing in Jeffrey Fairfax's twenty-five
years had prepared him for life aboard an
aircraft carrier in the South Pacific. His superb strength and fighting spirit nurtured
by ranch work and college football, then by
the rigorous U.S. Marine Corps training,
had failed to make ready his mind. Dying
held no fear for him. Possible capture, torture, and the niggling uncertainty as to how
much he could endure without showing
cowardice kept him awake when he needed
sleep. *Could any man withstand the atroci-
ties of war?*

In the darkest hours Jeff bared his soul,
faced himself, and set his course. With
God's help he would do a job he hated but
that must be done. When or if he came
home — he shrugged. Thinking of the
Laughing X now would make him soft when
he could least afford it.

He thought of his intensive training. He

remembered the way his stomach dropped while watching parachute practice and the involuntary tightening of his muscles when he breathlessly watched the chutes billow white against the sky and safely bring the men back to the earth. He fervently hoped he'd never have to jump. Flying was one thing; leaving the safety of the plane and leaping into thin air was something else.

Jeff's prior training with planes made him a perfect candidate for overseas duty. The weary looking superior officer who called him in introduced him to the captain with whom he'd fly.

"I wish we had thousands with your health and training," he said, then slammed a meaty fist onto the desk. "I'd go myself but the brass say I can do more here."

"I'll do my best, sir."

The heavy features relaxed in a comradely grin. "At ease, Marine. That's all any man can give."

Jeff and his senior pilot captain worked to-gether as easily as Jeff worked with Carson back in Montana. Mission after successful mission they flew, growing close in their shared tasks until Jeff loved his captain as a brother.

Weeks passed in a blur of fighting and driving the enemy back. One night when a hammered silver moon made grotesque shadows on land and sea, orders came for another attack.

"We're on mission to intercept southbound Japanese planes," the captain said. "It's going to be one grand ball, men. Choose your partners and hang on."

Jeff's skin crawled when they got underway. The smell of dying vegetation in the windless night crept through the open side window. The crash of sixteen-inch naval guns reached him even over the noise of their engines. Death filled the air. Below, fleets of small boats left foamy, white wakes. Tracers streaked toward shore. Smoke and high-flung earth and falling palm trees combined in a lurid haze. Nothing seemed real to Jeff except the quiet control of his aircraft commander. If he lived long enough to fly the countless missions his captain had flown, would he ever become so much a part of his plane?

Jeff looked down again and shuddered. The scene offered a foretaste of the prophesied biblical lake of fire. How could any man see this and still refuse to acknowledge the might and power of the living God?

"Captain, break left!" Jeff yelled when a Zero dove toward them. *Closer, closer.*

The commander dove, but the Japanese fighter stayed with them. Jeff felt cold sweat on his forehead. The plane shuddered when their gunners fired back. He heard the rattle of machine guns and knew the rest of the squadron was desperately trying to get the attacker.

Glass shattered. Splinters fell on Jeff's braced knees. The plane went into a crazy spin after a jolt that threatened to tear it apart.

The captain slumped, then straightened, and with a mighty effort righted the plane.

The intercom crackled. "We're hit, sir. Our tail's on fire," a disembodied voice warned. Acrid fumes filled the plane.

"How bad? Can you put it out?" Jeff yelled.

"We're trying."

The plane shuddered again. Jeff saw blood seep down his commander's face. "Sir, are you all right?"

"Fine," the grim-faced captain barked. "Our boys got him." He nodded toward the spiraling Zero that flamed down into the sea.

The intercom crackled again. "We can't stop it, sir. It's spreading and the enemy got our bombardier."

"We'll have to ditch." The commander

wasted no time. "But we'll get away from here first." He swung the crippled plane away from the land invasion and back out to sea. Only when the intercom informed him the fire had gone out of control did he order, "Ditching stations!"

Down, down, through a night gone strangely calm, in sharp contrast with the horrifying red light on land. Jeff's mind went blank.

"If I don't make it, you're in command," the captain said. His weak voice alerted his copilot that only sheer guts and will power had kept him going until the plane hit the water. Jeff snapped back to reality. What the Japanese hadn't done the tossing waves could do. The succession of events was bathed in confusion: throwing out the life raft, the crash into icy water, hoarse screaming, realizing his captain was beyond help, and dragging three of his crew members from the water to the life raft.

Praying as he had never done before, Jeff eyed the moon, wishing it would disappear. In its silver sheen the life raft made a grand target for any lone Japanese fighter plane that might have trailed them.

"And here he comes," Jeff muttered. "Hit the water. Stay under or float face down like you're dead."

The Zero swooped low, but evidently failed to see movement and, to the survivors' amazement, went on without raining bullets into their frail hope, the life raft.

"Curse this rotten war!" Jeff yelled after the departing Zero once it got nearly out of sight. Anger, grief, and salt water poured from his face. "God help those who gave their lives — and us."

Exhausted, the four marines huddled in the life raft, easy prey for the enemy and the elements. Two of those Jeff rescued died the second day. Dan Black, the radioman, and Jeff drifted, silent and thirsty in the middle of unlimited water.

For a week they drifted without compass or even one Allied plane to mark their plight. His tongue thick and swollen and lips cracked, reality and fantasy merged until at times Jeff didn't remember where he was. His companion suffered more from wounds he had received in the water. At the height of his delirium his ramblings sent cold shudders down Jeff's spine.

In late afternoon of the eighth day Jeff awoke from a dream of home. He'd been riding with Carson with the scent of pines and sage filling his lungs. "You can do it, boy," Carson kept encouraging.

Do what? Why did Carson keep telling

him that? And why did his own voice repeat over and over, "Too late, too late?"

Jeff's conscious state returned. His reddened eyes widened. Laughter that barely cackled in his dry throat rose and he shook his barely conscious buddy. "Wake up, fella, we're somewhere." His gaze never left the narrow beach toward which the life raft floated.

He got no response, only the feverish mutterings that showed how seriously ill the other man was.

"What shall I do?" he wondered in a voice too parched to carry. A dozen ideas came and fled. What new dangers lurked on the island ahead? How could he get there? Dehydrated and weak, could he swim if the tides turned against them? If he swam, what about the life raft and its precious cargo? Should he take a chance and shout? Should he just let the life raft drift in and make a run for it? If he stayed to help the wounded marine, would it mean capture for both?

The moment he had dreaded for weeks and months stared him in the face.

Jeff's soul swelled. No matter what the risk, he would not desert the only other survivor. The captain had put him in command. Well, he'd be the kind of commander the U.S. Marine Corps expected. Whatever lay ahead must come to both of them — or neither.

The capricious fate that had left them adrift in the ocean suddenly turned kind. Rocking waves brought them closer and closer to the island. Jeff squared his shoulders, sat erect, and waited.

Closer and closer, until only a few hundred yards remained between the life raft and the island. A hundred. Fifty. Thirty.

Out of an empty sky came the whine of planes. *Friend or enemy?* Jeff's keen, trained ears suspected the worst.

"Dear God, no!" His despairing prayer generated a bolt of energy beyond human strength. He leaped into the surf and cradled his companion with arms of steel. A lifetime ago and a world away he had been noted for his speed on the field. Now he ran with his heavy, mercifully unconscious burden, slowed by water to his waist but determined to go on fighting, head down.

Straight across the narrow beach he ran, to the dense growth ahead. Shouts reached his ears. Had he run into the arms of the enemy? Something exploded in his head. So the enemy had gotten him after all. He felt himself stumble and automatically threw out his arms. His buddy must fall clear or be crushed under Jeff's weight.

"Missed the touchdown," he whispered. "Someone tackled me." In a last convulsive effort, he felt a thrusting pain in his left side and crumpled to the ground.

Candleshine, Jane, Elizabeth, Magee, and the others settled into their routine. Days passed and communication still hadn't been established. Hopes of an early rescue faded. The soldiers chafed at the inactivity, wanting revenge for loss of the *Fortitude.* "How long are we gonna have to sit out here on this vacation spot?" they grumbled.

Magee responded by putting them to work improving living conditions. "If you guys don't start counting your blessings — like us not having neighbors and so far keeping out of sight and alive — I'm going to knock some heads together."

"Aw, Sarge, you know you're just as eager to get out of here and where we're needed as the rest of us."

"Yeah."

Candleshine heard the fighting spirit in his reply. The next instant he spoiled it by ordering, "Any man who gripes can do double watch duty." A loud groan followed.

Gradually the patients improved, even the young soldier and the second lieutenant. Candleshine and the others rejoiced. Magee offered to turn over command of No-Name Island but the nurses fixed the idea. "He's in no shape to do anything but get completely well," Elizabeth advised strongly. Jane and Candleshine backed her up. So Magee held the reins.

Never had Candleshine been treated so well. The men's appreciation and respect remained unlimited. They could fight and make home on the abandoned island but the three women represented healing. As soon as the last of the criticals won convalescent status, the two soldiers who had assisted in the first aid spelled the women.

Life was far better than Candleshine could have dreamed possible on the day they drifted in from the luckless *Fortitude*. Magee and his men found a secluded pool some distance from camp, cleared a trail, cleaned it out, and provided a bathing place. "Ladies when they want it, the rest of us other times," he ordered, scowling. "And if I catch any man around that pool when one of our nurses is there, I'll shoot him on sight."

A wave of protest rang through the assembly. "What kind of guys do you think we are?" someone yelled. "Anyone bothers our nurses, he'll wish the Japanese had got him!" Loud cheers followed.

Magee grinned. "See that you remember it. Dismissed."

Every day the nurses slipped away and bathed. The single change of clothing they'd been able to bring in the lifeboats could be washed, dried in the hot breezes, and worn the next day.

With more free time they could explore the tiny island. The men had already beaten down the brush and made rough paths that resembled tunnels beneath a green canopy.

Candleshine's favorite spot lay on the highest point of their little kingdom. Although it meant a climb, she loved the rocky knoll that overlooked the entire island.

"Make sure you keep outa sight if you ever see or hear a plane," Magee warned. A heavy crease between his eyebrows left no doubt of the seriousness of his concern. "It's not just your safety, but all of ours." He scratched his head and grunted. "So far we've been okay but I just don't know how long it will last."

"I'll be careful," she promised.

Sometimes Candleshine climbed with Jane or Elizabeth. Although soldiers begged to accompany her, most often she went alone. Something about the spot filled her need for solitude, a trait born and bred in her from Cedar Ridge. To draw apart for a time restored and freshened her. Once Magee teased, "If I didn't know better I'd think you rendezvoused with your fella up there. You come back bright and shiny and full of ginger."

She laughed at the crusty sergeant's teasing. They'd become great friends since they landed and she knew all about his wife and kids at home who waited and prayed for him to come back.

One afternoon after she and the other nurses straightened their quarters and left their two helpers in charge of the little hospital, Jane flopped to her bed. "My idea of heaven right now is a long, long nap and a good meal." She crossed her arms beneath her head. "I wonder if it will be fish and fruit or fruit and fish?"

"Who cares?" Elizabeth took off her shoes and placed them side by side in the precise way she did everything else. "I'm with you." She yawned. "Wonder when we all get home if we'll ever again be able to sleep without gunfire in the distance?" She lay back on her cot.

"I hope so. I don't intend to spend the rest of my life living next to a firing range," Jane sputtered. She glanced at their roommate. "Candleshine, are you taking a nap?"

She turned from the netting-clad opening

and smiled. "No, I'm restless today. I'll walk up to the lookout point."

"Again?" Jane smothered a yawn.

"I really love it up there." She retied her shoes and her blue eyes sparkled in her tanned face. "Have a good nap."

Mock snores followed her and she headed up the trail. Past the bathing pool the terrain became more steep. By the time she reached the tall trees used for lookouts she felt sweaty and hot but merely waved at the sentry who called to her and kept going. She'd have a swim and bath when she returned. Even her fair hair felt dirty and damp. She giggled and told a brilliant-plumed bird, "I never really thought Sergeant Magee could cut my hair with his knife but he did a pretty good job. Something to tell my grandkids!"

The thought sobered her and a few minutes later she sat down on the island's topknot. "Dear God, will I ever get married and have kids and grandkids? Sometimes it feels we've been here forever." Her unseeing eyes gazed at the beauty around her but her mind didn't register as usual. From meditation to blankness she let herself drift. The afternoon waned and she reluctantly stood, stretched, and started back down.

When she reached the sentry tree, she

couldn't believe what she saw. A half-dozen soldiers had gathered and stood staring out to sea. "What is it?"

"Look!" The speaker kept his voice low.

Candleshine had to strain her eyes to make out something low floating toward shore.

"It's a life raft," the sentry told them. "Can't tell, yes, there's something or someone in it. One of you guys go tell Magee and move it! The rest of you get your weapons, just in case. It could be a trap."

Candleshine's feet moved of their own accord. She raced down the path and past the beckoning pool that had lost its lure. Her heart pounded. She heard herself panting as she burst into camp. Jane stuck her head out of the tent, her eyes filled with sleep.

"Not one of you is to show himself — herself," Magee bellowed. "Until we know what that is, this is just a nice little deserted island, got it? But be prepared." He snapped a look at Candleshine and Jane. "Whatever happens, *stay down.* We don't want stray bullets picking off our nurses. Where's the other one?"

"Sound asleep." Jane giggled nervously. "She said she was so tired it would take a cannon to wake her."

"Let her sleep then. *Now get down!*"

The nurses obeyed, but picked a spot where they could see the water clearly. On both sides of them and in front the men crouched and lay low. Each carried whatever weapon he had and, in a few cases, that weapon was merely a heavy club.

Candleshine could see clearly now. A dark figure sat upright on the floating raft and something long and blanketed stayed motionless at his feet.

"I think he's one of ours but we can't be sure," someone whispered and earned a black scowl from Magee.

In the distance the sound of planes preceded them. Jane's nails dug into Candleshine's arm. Tiny drops of sweat beaded on her nose.

A second later the seated figure scrambled from the life raft, snatched the inert burden, and ran toward the hidden island inhabitants. Head down, still his height showed clearly.

"That ain't no Jap," Magee shouted. "Watch it, buddy!"

His warning came too late. In an effort to find cover before the enemy discovered them, the runner had plowed head-on into the jungle foliage. A heavy branch, dislodged by the impact, snapped forward and struck his head.

"Help him, men! Get that raft under cover and blot out the traces." Magee and the others, spurred by danger of discovery and death for all, leaped to their feet.

So did the nurses. Before they could take a single step forward, the soaked, unshaven man in a marine uniform faltered. To Candleshine's horrified, fascinated gaze the way he thrust his burden ahead of him then buckled resembled slow motion. She saw the pain in his face. His lips moved. He twisted and another spasm of agony crossed his thin face before he lay still.

Candleshine jerked free of Jane's painful grip and pelted toward the two downed men. "Get Elizabeth," she cried. "And our aides." Twice she caught her foot in roots and almost fell but reached the newcomers before either moved. All her experience rose in a hasty examination of the blanketed man. When her trained fingers discovered the crudely bandaged wounds, she ordered, "Get him to the hospital," glad for Magee's ingenuity that had prepared for disaster by making stretchers of bamboo stems and blankets.

The runner lay as he had fallen. Candleshine stanched the flow of blood from his head with pressure from the heel of her hand. "Turn him toward me, but be careful," she instructed Magee. "Head wounds always bleed a lot."

"He must have fallen on something sharp," Magee said when they got the marine turned. He jerked open the dirty shirt. A gaping hole oozed blood.

"It isn't as bad as it looks," Candleshine rejoiced and directed Magee how to stop the blood. "He's going to have one big headache from that lump and we'll have to watch his side, but he should be all right."

Did the prone man hear her voice? He stirred, struggled against their restraining hands, and at last opened his eyes. Staring straight into Candleshine's face, etched against the fading sunlight, he licked his salty, cracked lips.

"Am I dead? Are you an angel?" He tried to sit up, but flinched and fell back into unconsciousness.

Nine

Candleshine had cared for hundreds of patients during her career, and dozens of them had fallen in love with her. A few had stirred a faint interest inside her but that was always driven away by her desire not to care about any man until the war ended.

Now one glimpse of eyes so dark she thought they were black but later discovered were clear, deep blue and the whispered words, "Am I dead? Are you an angel?" lighted a tiny flame in her heart. Fear shot through her when the pallid marine fell back unconscious. "Get him to the hospital," she ordered, and ran ahead to whisk a blanket on one of the cots, vacant now that her other patients had healed.

Elizabeth, refreshed from her afternoon nap, greeted them. Never had Candleshine been more thankful for the older nurse's advanced skills. Elizabeth stitched wounds as carefully as the finest doctor.

Her firm, gentle hands sought and bathed the jagged gash in the man whose dog tag identified him as Lieutenant Jeffrey Fairfax.

"Nice name. When he heals and gets over the effects of exposure he will be as good-looking as ever." Elizabeth cast a sharp glance at Candleshine who hovered near. "I don't like that goose egg on his head so I want you to watch him." She washed her hands in hot water and disinfectant. "Now for the other poor devil dog."

Candleshine remained by Lieutenant Fairfax's cot but heard Jane's quickly muffled gasp when Elizabeth exposed the second marine's chest.

"It's going to take a lot more than time and good food to restore this one," Elizabeth muttered matter of factly. "Fairfax did all he could and probably saved his buddy's life but we've got to reopen the wounds so they'll heal from the inside out. Thank God both of them stayed unconscious until we could do our jobs."

An hour later she straightened. "That will do it. The warm air can help heal."

Time off for the three nurses vanished. Lieutenant Fairfax and his radioman, Dan Black, tossed and turned and relived the events preceding their watery plunge. From parched lips and fevered brains, Magee and the nurses got the whole story, and marveled that any man from the ditched plane had survived. Candleshine spent most of her night shift trotting between Fairfax and Black. If her gaze lingered longer on the lieutenant than on the radioman only the mosquitoes knew.

For two days and nights Black's life hung by a cobweb. Jane forgot her dislike of night duty and specialed the young marine, forcing water between his tightly clenched lips when she could and sponging away the rivers of sweat. "Don't be alarmed when he sweats hard," Elizabeth had warned. "It helps get the poison out of his system and the fever itself burns up infection."

Candleshine stayed with Fairfax who alternated between growing periods of consciousness and restless sleep. One night he violently jerked from her ministering hands. "No, Lillian! Just leave me alone."

"All right." Candleshine used the low but penetrating voice she employed to penetrate mental confusion.

"I won't do it. Uncle Sam says come. Think I'd leave the Laughing X for a desk job?" He strained to sit up and Candleshine gently pressed him back.

"You don't have to, Jeffrey." The name

felt good on her lips the first time she used it. "No one will make you."

He grunted. His lean face twisted and his eyes opened. "You — you're not Lillian." Some of the fever receded and recognition filled his eyes. "You're the angel. You won't let her —"

"Don't try to talk," she ordered and reached for a cloth. She dipped it in cool water and bathed his face.

"Where am I, anyway?" Jeffrey Fairfax slowly turned his head, surveyed the dimly lit ward, and picked at the light blanket with nervous fingers. "I didn't know they had bananas in heaven."

Candleshine started, then realized his wandering gaze had lighted on the eternal bunch of bananas Magee kept on hand for quick energy for the nurses. "No bananas in heaven," she told him. "We'll talk about it tomorrow."

"Okay, angel." The tall body relaxed and a little later Candleshine noted with satisfaction his deep and evidently dreamless sleep so in contrast with the frenzied periods of unconsciousness.

"Lieutenant Fairfax is much better," she reported to Elizabeth the next morning. A lilt in her voice matched the sparkle in her blue eyes.

"Good. Get some breakfast and sleep as long as you can," she advised. "You, too," she told a weary Jane. The nurses could barely stay awake long enough to eat. But before they went to their quarters, they trudged to the bathing pool and came back with lifted spirits.

"Dan is improving but I just don't know." Jane's somber face showed her concern. "I wish we could get off this island and to Australia or Guadalcanal or anywhere!" Unaccustomed tears spilled and she impatiently brushed them away. "I know," she told Candleshine. "We're not supposed to get emotionally involved with our patients. I don't. Ever. But Dan is so much like the brother I lost. . . ." Her lips quivered.

"Would you like to trade patients?" Candleshine offered, wondering why a little disappointment filled her at the idea.

"If it's all right with Elizabeth." Jane flung herself to her cot. Moments later she slept, more emotionally than physically exhausted in spite of the drain of strength used in caring for the late arrivals.

Elizabeth readily agreed to the switch when Candleshine privately explained and that night the nurses changed places in the little ward. Candleshine looked at the wasted form of Dan Black and echoed

Jane's prayer. *How could they take care of him here when he needed the best possible attention?* Limited by dwindling medical supplies and crude conditions, Candleshine turned to her Heavenly Father in prayer, asking for mercy and guidance.

Once that night Lieutenant Fairfax roused and whispered, "Where's the angel?"

Jane looked astonished but told him, "Right over there taking care of your radio-man."

The answer seemed to satisfy him and he fell back asleep but Jane sent an impish grin across the barely lighted ward and raised one eyebrow. Candleshine felt rich color creep from her collar into her face.

A week later Lieutenant Fairfax had regained full control of his mental state and voracious appetite and, except for a sore head and side, had mended to the point of examining the encampment. He praised Magee, declined to take command at this time, and never let Nurse Thatcher out of sight when he could help it.

How much broken memory was real? He vaguely remembered her cool hands doing their healing work, her attractive face close when she cared for him. Once he asked, "Did I mumble?"

A wide smile lighted Candleshine's face.

"Oh, yes." She couldn't help but tease a little even though something in his eyes caught her breath.

"What did I say?" He watched her capable hands mending a rip in one of the men's khaki shirts.

"You called for Lillian."

"Never!" His eyes flashed. His lips thinned. For a moment his face lost its peaceful look and turned dark.

"You talked about a laughing x and a desk job," she informed him.

His shout of laughter brought color to her face and the quick gaze of every person in sight. Jeff settled more comfortably against the tree trunk where he'd found Candleshine working. "It's not *a* laughing x but *the* Laughing X. A cattle ranch in western Montana."

"Really?" The mending dropped to Candleshine's lap in a forgotten pile. "A real, live cattle ranch with horses and roundups and —"

"— and bunkhouse and ranchhouse and corrals," he added solemnly.

She bit her lip. "You're laughing at me."

"Not really. You just sounded so surprised."

His keen gaze confused her. "Well, what would you think? Here a marine lieutenant comes calling, we bring him back to health, and it turns out he's really a cowboy!"

Jeff's boyish grin contrasted sharply with the tiny patches of silver that hadn't graced his dark hair a few weeks earlier. "Rancher too. I own the place. If we ever get out of this hole and back home, would you like to visit the Laughing X? The other nurses, too," he hastily added.

She liked him for that addition. "I'd love to," she said in the simple, honest way that left no room for misunderstanding. "We live in a beautiful part of the country. Cedar Ridge in the mountains of Washington State can't be beat. But I've always been crazy about western history." Excitement made her blue eyes even bluer.

"I can show you a lot when you come," he told her.

Again she felt color steal into her face. He hadn't said *if* but **when.** The very thought made her heart beat faster.

Jeff half-closed his eyes and started talking. "The wide spaces, the smell of pine and sage, the mountains in the distance — sometimes I'd give everything I own to be back. Even the hard work and isolation in bad winters are worth it. My foreman Carson's back there right now raising beef for the government. He's fighting his battles, too, trying to get enough riders to do the job and hampered by the lack of skill." His lips curved reminiscently. "We don't hire any man who won't start the naturalization process."

"I don't blame you." Candleshine bent her head and went back to her mending. *How much this marine resembled Dad in character and outlook!*

"Just where is this Cedar Ridge? I have to confess I've never heard of it."

Candleshine's fingers stilled. "Forty miles east of Bellingham. Cedar Ridge is in a valley between mountains, like the bottom of a teacup." A flood of memories roughened her voice.

"How did you end up a million miles from it?"

In brief, revealing sentences she shared how she and her cousin had vowed to make a team. She told him about Mercy Hospital and Training School, Hunter Hall, Bruce and Winona and Connie, Miss Grey, Sally, and the others. She lightly touched on her determination to carry the torch her great-grandmother had passed down and that she would faithfully keep lighted.

"It isn't easy sometimes," she said in a voice so low Jeff had to lean close to hear. "I — I'm not a very brave person." She hesitated. *Could she tell him about her faith in God and how only that helped her get through the rough times?*

Before she could continue, Jeff said, "My parents felt the same way. Their motto for living was that everyone owed the world the best they could give."

In the change of conversation, Candleshine's opportunity to witness slipped by.

Gradually, and to the chagrin of the other island inhabitants who vied for her attentions, Candleshine spent more and more of her free time with Jeff. Long before she knew he had fallen in love with her, she lay awake when she should be sleeping and thought of him. Somewhere along the way her solid determination never to allow herself to care for any man in wartime had melted.

"He isn't just *any* man," she whispered brokenly when at last she honestly admitted to herself the love in her heart. Next to God, Lieutenant Jeffrey Fairfax possessed her love.

A little frown crossed her face and she shifted uneasily. They had so little uninterrupted time! Each time she had gathered her courage to ask how he felt about God and if he knew Jesus, something happened to stop the words on her lips.

Deteriorating conditions on the island added to her troubled state. Japanese planes patrolled daily. *Had they seen something?* No one knew for sure, but when bombs fell Magee called the entire company together and laid everything before them. Every trace of his good nature had fled in the face of necessity.

"We're running short of food, believe it or not. We still have some fruit and fish when we can catch them but we can't hold out forever. The Japanese have to be suspicious or they wouldn't be wasting time and bombs. From now on, either sleep in your helmets or have them next to your cots. Hit the trenches every time you hear planes. The one good thing is that we've been able to make contact. Our people know we're here but they're a little busy just now and can't be running a shuttle service to Guadal." He glared at the innocent-looking waves playing on the beach. "Keep out of sight even when you don't think there's any reason. Dismissed."

Candleshine took a deep breath, more from what he'd left unsaid than his actual orders. If they were invaded it meant capture and who knew what?

Yet in the momentous, waiting days even fear could not dampen her growing love for Jeff. A hundred times she glanced up and met his poignant gaze. She saw the longing in his face to speak and the rigid self-discipline that kept him silent. Did he feel as she often did that love born in the middle of fear could not survive? That it was too soon, too fast?

One early evening she climbed with him to the rocky point on top of the island. Mindful of Magee's orders, they didn't step into the open but observed their world from cover provided by the heavy growth.

"I never seriously cared for any girl," Jeff said out of the blue. "I was always too busy. . . . until now."

Had she really heard the almost inaudible words? Candleshine felt herself blush as she had long ago the first time a boy sat with her in the little Cedar Ridge church. She turned toward him.

"I love you, Candleshine Thatcher. Will you marry me?" His blue eyes looked black with emotion. "I wasn't going to say anything. It didn't seem fair. But with the Japanese getting closer all the time. . . ."

She couldn't bear the pain in his face. "I —"

Jeff gripped her hands until they ached. His look burned into her soul. "Just knowing you love me, that you'll be my wife, you can't know what a difference it will make!"

He drew her close and pressed her cheek against his shoulder then kissed her.

Candleshine's hands crept up his shoulders and clasped behind his head. She returned his kiss with all the love that had stormed and seized her heart in spite of everything she could do to lock it. "I'll marry you, Jeff."

"When?"

"Why, as soon as we can."

He kissed her again, this time joyously. When he released her and held her at arm's length all signs of stress had flown. His dark blue eyes laughed into her own and his white teeth gleamed in his bronzed face. "The minute we get to Guadalcanal or to wherever we can find someone with authority, we'll hunt him up." A shadow crossed his face. "That is, if we can get permission." Doubt sponged some of his gladness before the same indomitable will that kept him and Dan Black alive against impossible odds came to his rescue again. "They'll have to give it!" He pulled her back into his arms and sealed his promises with a tender kiss. "Shall we tell everyone?"

The first twinge of alarm sounded deep in Candleshine's brain. Released from the security of Jeff's strong arms Candleshine felt dazed.

"On second thought," he suggested, observing her confused stare, "let's just keep it to ourselves. It's too precious to share just now."

Relief filled her and the feeling she'd been given a reprieve. Yet cradled against his shoulder Candleshine found it hard to think beyond the moment and savored the sweetness that had so unexpectedly fallen.

Before they reached camp Jeff stopped her and held her close. "I'll never stop giving thanks for your love." The next instant he decorously followed her along the well-trod path. He saluted smartly for the benefit of curious eyes. "Thank you for the walk, Nurse Thatcher."

"You're welcome, lieutenant." She blindly watched him stride away, every inch the trained marine and somehow not quite the Jeff who had opened his heart on top of the island.

That night when Candleshine had done everything she could for Dan Black and found time dragging she brought out in the quiet ward every image of the afternoon engraved into her soul. She paced back and forth until at last she sank onto an empty cot and buried her face in her arms.

Dear God, what have I done? Promised to marry a man, to live as his wife — for-

ever. A man I have only known a few weeks, one I'm not sure believes in God, though little comments of his could mean otherwise.

"I can't do it," she breathed, feeling great drops of perspiration spring to her forehead.

Yet how can I back down? The cruelest thing on earth would be to go back on her word. She imagined Jeff's face if she told him how she felt. She could picture his scorn and disgust for a girl who committed herself then weaseled out with a lame excuse.

Torn, hurting, Candleshine sat for hours. A dozen ideas came and went, discarded as impossible. Never had she endured such a night. "Better to come forward than destroy two lives with a hasty marriage," she tried to tell herself but her mind and heart went black.

When Jane came to relieve her early the next morning she found Candleshine staring into the distance, unresponsive to Jane's greetings. The last thought Candleshine had before she finally fell asleep in her quarters haunted her dreams: What should she do?

She awakened to the roar of planes and the exploding of bombs. She snatched her helmet and zigzagged across to the nearest trench. Dirt erupted in little geysers on both sides of her. She saw running figures. Some fell. The instant the planes left she raced to the downed soldiers, selfishly glad Jeff hadn't been hit but ashamed at her relief. The hospital stood intact and although several men had been injured, none had been killed. Candleshine, Elizabeth, and Jane probed, bandaged, and beat back death.

Four hours later Magee burst into the ward. "We're getting out of here. Now. Get your men on stretchers — a couple of PT boats are on their way. It's risky but better than staying here like sitting ducks." His grim expression did nothing to reassure the nurses.

They made their way to the narrow beach by starlight, thankful for the dark phase of the moon. "Keep under cover until I tell you," Magee ordered in a low voice.

"Where are the lieutenants?" Candleshine clutched his arm.

"They and a few others are covering our rear," Magee snapped. "Fine time for them to take command." Anger laced his hoarse whisper. "I should be the guy staying behind."

"What do you mean?" Candleshine felt sick.

"Somebody's got to do it. They'll run for

the PT boats at the last minute, after everyone else is on." He dismissed the others in concern for the wounded. "Are you ready when I give the signal?"

"Yes." Elizabeth stood close and Jane protectively patted Dan Black's hand. He had come back from the edge of death but needed more time to heal totally.

"Shhh. Here they come." Magee loomed big in the semidarkness and peered into the ocean.

Candleshine's gaze followed. Would any of them be spared? A surprise attack was always a possibility either while they boarded or in the open water between No-Name Island and Guadalcanal.

Her heart lifted in prayer, she crouched next to the stretcher patients and strained her eyes toward the oncoming PT boats, desperately longing for Jeff and the others to appear.

Ten

"Why did *two* PT boats come?" Candle-shine whispered, muscles tense. She was ready to run. "There aren't enough of us to crowd just one."

"Probably as cover," Elizabeth mur-mured in her ear. "If one is hit, at least some of us will get out alive, we hope." She pressed Candleshine's hand, then Jane's. "Just in case we don't all survive, you're the finest nurses I've ever worked beside."

Candleshine couldn't have answered if she'd had time. Such high praise from this veteran nurse meant so much. In the heart-beat between Elizabeth's whisper and Magee's order to run for the PT boats, the young nurse cringed inwardly and won-dered. What would Elizabeth say if she knew Candleshine had promised to marry Lieutenant Fairfax and now quivered with cowardice and shame?

The long-awaited and dreaded evacuation took fifteen minutes. Magee separated the group and Candleshine shuddered, remembering what Elizabeth had said. The older nurse ordered Jane and Candleshine to go together and calmly saw to the loading of the stretcher patients. The rear guard joined the evacuees after satisfying themselves that so far no Japanese fighter planes had discovered the unusual activity on the beach. Lieutenant Fairfax gave a final sweeping to the narrow strip.

Candleshine's fears subsided when he boarded the PT boat and came to where she knelt by a wounded soldier. At least he'd be close if the evacuation turned into a nightmare.

Elizabeth called guardedly from the other PT boat, "See you in Guadalcanal!" Their last sight of the gallant woman was a wave in the starlight before the PT boat swung back toward open water. Candleshine looked back at No-Name Island only once. Dark and silent, from their position it looked as untouched as it had so long ago when the weary survivors from the *Fortitude* sought its shelter. The stripped fruit trees and a deserted camp would be the only indications of a human refuge.

"This little mosquito boat can sting the enemy — it's deadly in the dark," Magee told the nurses in barely discernible tones. "We may just get out of here yet."

For a time his prophecy proved true. No familiar hum that grew into the ugly whine of enemy planes marred the still darkness. No enemy warships loomed. Candleshine dared to breathe normally, until an explosion ahead shot bursts of orange flame into the velvet night.

"Dear God!" Jeff grabbed Candleshine and hid her face against his chest but not before the fiery scene was engraved in her mind.

She clung to him. "The other boat?"

"Torpedoed." His arms tightened around her. "I thought all the Japanese subs in this area had been detected and destroyed. One must have sneaked past our surveillance."

Candleshine tore free from his protective hold. "Why are we changing course? Why, we're running away!" Her voice rose to a shriek and anger burned out fear. "Why aren't we going to help, to pick up survivors? Elizabeth — the others —"

"There are no survivors." His burning eyes penetrated deep into hers. Yet her protests could not be quelled.

"You don't know that!" she cried wildly. "Magee, tell him." She licked dry lips. *"We can't just leave."*

Magee said hoarsely, "PT boats carry 5000 pounds of explosives."

His defeated face sent red-hot pokers of pain into her but she took a deep breath, held it, and submitted to a dull acceptance.

In a wild series of maneuvers, the PT boat fled, leaving part of Candleshine buried in the waters between No-Name Island and Guadalcanal. Even Jeff's reassurance that Allied planes would get the sub now that it had been located didn't penetrate the numbness that settled on her like a rain-soaked tarpaulin. Candleshine never knew how long it took to reach Guadalcanal. She barely responded to the welcoming cheers of the military personnel who held the reclaimed island. Only the needs of the men she cared for kept her going. She had seen men die in war and in civilian life. But to witness what she had had drained her magnificent strength.

For a full week Jeff observed her, knowing only too well her pain and the wall she erected to keep out more hurt. In a bold effort to smash the threat to her mental health, he drew her aside one day. "Candleshine, there's a chaplain here. You promised to marry me. If I can get permission, will you? Here? Now? Who knows what the future will allow?"

She came out of her fog and despair. *Why not take what happiness she could when it could be all there was?* Why let hesitation and thoughts of the future stop them? What if she didn't know him well? Having his strength to draw from helped her go on.

A fine, white line circled Jeff's lips. His midnight blue eyes searched hers. "I'm almost well. I'll be sent back to active duty soon." He cleared the huskiness from his voice. "At least we'd have a few days of heaven first."

She closed her eyes and remembered the security of his arms that night in the PT boat. Tomorrow and the next day dimmed. A single nod of her head would give them today.

"Nurse Thatcher," Magee's voice separated them. "You're needed." His stocky body followed his voice. "Oh, sorry, lieutenant."

Jeff just grunted before turning glowing eyes on Candleshine. "Don't forget what I said."

As if she could! God, help me, she prayed. *I'm too tired to fight any longer.* She watched Jeff walk away, wondering if his meeting with a superior officer at the edge of the compound meant anything. Or the way his radioman Dan Black joined them.

Magee motioned for Candleshine and Jane to step to one side. His troubled gaze moved from one to the other. "I need one of you to accompany a patient to Australia," he said bluntly. "The medics say one of our boys who got hit in that last little episode on No-Name Island has to have better care than we can give him here. A medic can't be spared, so one of you is it."

Candleshine's heart raced. *Could this be God's way of answering her prayer by giving her time away to think?* She looked at Jane. "Do you want me to go?"

"It may be dangerous." Jane bit her lip. "I can go." Yet the look she cast in Dan Black's direction gave away her longing to stay.

"The way I see it," Magee began as he had done so many times before, "there's no real safety guaranteed here or anywhere." He scratched his head and Candleshine felt a tide of friendship for the big, rough staff sergeant.

"I'll go. How soon do I need to be ready?"

"Four hours ago." Magee grimaced. "Grab what you can and meet me back here in fifteen minutes." He saluted them, marched off, and came back five minutes later to find Candleshine almost ready. "You're going, too," he told Jane. "Orders from headquarters."

She stared, then set her jaw and started packing. Suddenly she stopped. "I have to see someone before I go."

"So do I." Candleshine crammed the rest of her stuff together.

"You've got five minutes," Magee warned. "Hurry up the goodbyes."

Dan Black stood nearby and Jane rushed to him. Candleshine raced after her. "Lieutenant Fairfax, where is he?"

Dan jerked his head toward the far side of the compound. His kind eyes looked sad and aware. "High-powered meeting with the brass."

"But I must see him!"

"Sorry, Nurse Thatcher. No one interrupts such meetings unless it's life or death." Pity softened his face. "I'll deliver a message when I can."

Half sobbing, Candleshine hurried back and found paper and pencil. Tears stained the page and she barely got it into an envelope before Magee called, "Time's up."

Dan and Jane had crossed to them, their hands linked. Jane grabbed her things and Candleshine pressed the envelope in Dan's outstretched hand. "Tell him . . . tell him. . . ." She couldn't go on.

For the sake of those they served, the nurses held back their own feelings. As

Magee had said, this was war. Partings, fear, and service were all part of the deadly hide-and-seek game between those who sought to destroy and those who maintained freedom.

Candleshine thought of her hastily scribbled message. *When would Jeff get it? How would he feel?* She couldn't think about it. She must carry on, even as he would carry on. Something in Dan Black's eyes had warned how important the high-powered meeting would be to his future and Jeff's. Perhaps even now the two men were throwing things together as the nurses had done, preparing to leave on new flying assignments. Would Jeff understand the real meaning behind her words? Or would he see them for what they were, a desperate grab for a life raft of escape from marriage to him?

I've been ordered to Australia with the wounded. It will give me time to think. God bless and keep you. Candleshine.

Weeks later Candleshine lay as a patient in the same Australian hospital she, Jane, and the others had reached after leaving Guadalcanal. Instead of caring for others, she chafed at her own inactivity.

"You're going home," Jane announced one day.

"What?" Candleshine started to sit up but Jane grimly pushed her back down.

"Heavens, what terrible patients nurses make! I said that you're going home. No use arguing. The doctor says you're a victim of battle fatigue on top of malaria." Jane scowled. "How could you have forgotten to take your Atabrine?"

Candleshine felt tears of weakness slide down her nose. "If you remember correctly, we were involved in some pretty hectic times." Her voice trembled and she turned her head away.

"I'm sorry," Jane quickly said. She smoothed the younger nurse's pillow. "Don't you see, though, unless you're able to help care for others you —"

"— I'm just an added burden," Candleshine finished bitterly. "What a way to end up my war efforts, flat on my back when you and every other nurse here is run off her feet!"

"Just be glad we got here," Jane quietly reminded. She sighed and cocked her head to one side. The grin that made her so popular among her patients crept out. "Frankly, I'd give a month's pay to trade places with you now that the chills and fever are over. I could use the rest." She yawned.

"Jane, have you heard anything from Dan Black?"

"No." The word hung between them. "If things work out, someday, well, he knows where to find me." She brushed aside personal concerns and stretched tired muscles, "I have work to do." She patted Candleshine's hand. "I keep believing he's all right." She sighed again and a faraway look touched her eyes. "It's all I — or any girl who loves a marine — can do." Jane slipped out of sight.

Candleshine repeated to herself what Jane had said. She closed her eyes. Love that made her ache filled her heart and mind but guilt had the last word. Not only had she run from a promise, she had failed to witness of her Lord to a man who faced death every time he went out on a mission.

Did Jeff know God? Had he accepted Jesus? Candleshine couldn't be sure. She only knew that the precious moments they had spent talking of themselves, their love, and their dreams had failed to include the most important topic of all. If Jeff were killed in action, she would never know whether he'd been a Christian. Could she bear the cross of uncertainty?

Will and Trinity Thatcher openly rejoiced when they learned their only daughter had been ordered home. Surely Cedar Ridge would help erase whatever she had experienced in the long months overseas. Yet when they picked her up in Seattle, pale, aloof, and strangely haunted, Trinity could barely stand to look at her. The imprint of her service had left an indelible mark. Where had Candleshine gone? Who was this stranger that sat between them and gazed out the window with eyes that neither saw nor cared? Physically rundown, the light that once made Candleshine far more attractive than her features had flickered so low Trinity wondered if it still existed.

Months passed. Candleshine's superb health slowly returned. Regardless of the weather, she spent as much time outside as possible, reveling in the crispness of a world away from tropical heat. Yet a shadow remained in her eyes and her parents worried and prayed harder than ever.

Five times she traveled to Mercy Hospital in Seattle and begged Miss Grey to put her back to work. Five times Miss Grey sighed over how badly she needed Candleshine and denied the request. "Not until *I* feel you are ready," she said through lips made even grimmer by the war years.

"How will you — or I — know?"

"I'll know." Miss Grey's lips relaxed. "So will you."

In late fall 1944 Candleshine climbed to the spot where she and Bruce had dreamed and planned a lifetime before. A growing fever inside her demanded action, not this silly recuperating business everyone insisted she have. How much time off did Jane or Miss Grey, Connie, Bruce, or Winona have? Or Jeff. . . .

Her blue eyes darkened. Sometimes Jeff and their love seemed like a dream or from such a shrouded past that it slipped away in the mists. Was he still alive? Did he remember the woman who promised to marry him? The dagger in her soul turned and pierced her to the core.

"Dear God, if I could only feel free." The desire for relief from her heavy burden welled inside her and spilled into the late autumn day. Time after time Will and Trinity had given her the opportunity to speak but something inside her froze the words.

Now she cried, "Dear Heavenly Father, give me strength to tell them what happened over there and to rid myself of this specter. My skills are needed but my torch has burned so low I can't serve. Please, God, help me."

An hour later she stood, walked back to her home, and took a deep breath. "I have a story to tell you."

She began with her early fears about turning coward in the face of disaster. She relived the panic of fleeing from the sinking *Fortitude* and spared no detail concerning the time that followed: the drifting; sighting the island and wondering if the Japanese held it; living under a cloud of perpetual vigilance lest they be discovered.

Strangely enough, when it came to the arrival of Lieutenant Fairfax and his radioman she said little except that they needed care. Something inside her shrank from exposing even to these two how she felt. If Jeff ever came home, it would be time to share.

With clenched hands and glazed eyes she again boarded the PT boat. Even when she told how the Japanese submarine made a direct torpedo hit on the other boat she didn't flinch.

Once Trinity stirred in protest, appalled at the look in her daughter's face. Will's warning glance riveted her to her chair and silenced her. She sank back, suffering with Candleshine but realizing it must all come out before healing could occur.

Dinner forgotten, Candleshine talked

until her voice came out in a croak and evening gloom crept into the living room. She stopped, emptied.

"My darling girl!" Trinity could stand no more. She reached out both arms.

Like a sleepwalker coming out of a long period of unconsciousness, she stumbled across the room and fell to her knees with her head in her mother's lap. Great tearing sobs came, washing away the painful remembrances of an unimaginable past.

"Steady, little girl," Will's broken voice said. "It's all over now. You're here and you're safe."

Except for the one, long splinter in her heart, her love for Jeff, Candleshine felt remade.

Two days later she stood in Miss Grey's office, impeccable in her Mercy Hospital white uniform and black-banded cap. "I'm ready for orders."

A lightning glance from the famous gray eyes, a slow smile, and warm handshake were evidence her time again had come. Miss Grey said, "We need you in rehabilitation. Can you handle it?"

"Yes."

"Thank God." Miss Grey rose, not in the old way that reduced her probationers to quivering jelly, but awkwardly, with weariness in every motion. "Welcome home, Candleshine."

Tested and found to be pure gold in the fires of war, Candleshine brought to the droves of soldiers necessary physical rehabilitation and the gentle firmness that encouraged them beyond themselves. Someone had told them her story and the servicemen took her to their hearts. Anyone who had been under fire in the Pacific theater knew about nightmares and that tears did not always mean weakness. To make up for the months of recuperation when she had nothing to give, Candleshine now worked long hours uncomplainingly and never failed to let the nurses she supervised know how valuable they were.

Sally Monroe had gone overseas as she predicted. New faces filled the wards and halls. Yet Mercy Hospital and Training School continued an important cog in winning the war on the home front.

Although Candleshine never neglected a patient or gave one more care than another, she found herself especially drawn to those coming home from the Pacific. Whenever opportunities arose, she quietly asked, "Did you ever run across a marine lieutenant named Jeffrey Fairfax?" Yet after many weeks the only response was "Sorry." She also asked after Dan Black but the answer remained the same, each time leaving her empty but determined to do all she could to locate Jeff. Even if he despised her for running away, she owed him an explanation, and her witness of Christ.

Early in 1945 encouraging war news drifted back. United States and the Allied forces had liberated island after island from the Japanese. The New Guinea and Central Pacific campaigns had brought the Allies within striking distance of the Philippines several months earlier. In late October 1944 General MacArthur kept his pledge to return, but only after more than two years of costly fighting. The battle for Leyte Gulf in late October ended in a major victory for the Allies. The remaining Japanese navy no longer posed a threat.

Yet the continuing battle for Leyte that ran through 1944 brought perhaps the most chilling weapon Japan offered, the *kamikaze*. These "suicide pilots" crashed planes filled with explosives into Allied warships, unless shot down before they crashed. Candleshine set her lips, prayed the madness would end, and continued her own work, always hoping of news about Jeff. *How long could it go on,* she wondered. The very word kamikaze, which means "divine wind," stilled even the most talkative patients. How much the world needed Christ, with His message of unconditional love! Why couldn't Japan see they had no chance of winning?

In early March news came that Manila had been retaken by the Allies. A burly soldier due to be released caught Candleshine around the waist and swung her off her feet into a wild victory dance. All her protests meant nothing.

The whole rehabilitation ward chanted, "Manila's ours, Manila's ours," until Candleshine pressed her hands over her ears. Even the doctor couldn't dim the spirit of hope that had built from early January when the Allies landed on Luzon.

"Sure, and it's about over," the burly soldier shouted. "They can't last much longer!"

Their contagious joy fired Candleshine's heart. Her torch indeed flared bright. God willing, the long, dark months would end and brightness would return. In the meantime, her body and soul must continue in service; more men would come home and many would need her skills.

She adjusted her cap and went back to work.

Eleven

"Captain Fairfax?"

"Yes, sir?" Jeff stood with pantherlike grace and saluted.

"First, congratulations on your new rank. From what I hear, you've earned it. At ease," the hatchet-faced major barked. "Have a chair."

Jeff relaxed as much as the straight-backed office chair permitted. "Thanks." He eyed his superior officer.

"I understand you're due for leave." Keen eyes bored into Jeff's brain, but the younger marine's lips thinned.

"Due but I don't want it, sir. We've been flying successful missions and we have the Japanese on the run. I need every pilot who can handle a plane." Jeff laughed. "Why am I telling you this, sir? You know more about it than I do."

"I do."

Jeff's mouth twitched. The major sounded

like a participant in a wedding, a thought that made Jeff's heart lurch.

The major leaned forward from behind his battered desk. "Manila is in rubble. Our massive incendiary raid has destroyed the heart of Tokyo." The gruff major cleared his throat. "Approximately 25,000 of our marines died or were wounded in taking Iwo Jima. Our B-29 bombers have been pounding Japan's industries and our subs sinking the supplies they need so badly. We've got them on the run but at a terrible cost." A gray shade dropped like a visor over his lean face. "Okinawa, 50,000 Allied casualties."

Jeff's heart went out to the major. "Yes, sir. But every one of those men believed in what he did."

"It's the only thing that helps me stay sane." The major's eyes flamed. "Captain, if the world doesn't learn this time that war is more than a deadly game, I don't know what will happen. What lies ahead is worse than the past. If the Allies invade Japan itself, we could lose a million Americans alone! But I didn't call you in to discuss strategy. We have enough generals and colonels for that. Do I understand correctly that you are officially turning down the leave I was ordered to offer?"

"Yes, sir."

The major rose. "I'd do the same." He stretched a surprisingly strong hand out and the man behind the officer smiled. "Carry on, and thank you. Dismissed."

Jeff's eyes stung. He returned the grip and saluted, then turned smartly on his heel and marched out. All the heroes weren't on the front lines. Without being told, Jeff knew his major would give everything to be in the cockpit of an attacking plane instead of ordering others to go from behind a desk.

What would this summer of 1945 bring? More death and destruction? So far he had been spared, but how many more times could he get back to base when other planes in his squadron spiraled into flames? Jeff brushed his hand over his eyes to blot out those memories.

War stories raced like wildfire through his mind. When the army mop-up boys landed at Subic Bay, unloaded arms, and prepared to put the finishing touches on Japanese resistance, even aerial support couldn't suppress the danger. Neither did the support artillery that laid a ring of steel around them. Holding a position could be a nightmare. Every shadow or movement demanded attention from men so fatigued night came as an enemy instead of a time to rest. One soldier on watch saw two unknown entities "creeping up" the trail. He put a bullet in each. They turned out to be trees.

Another soldier whose weight had gone down to 160 pounds staggered under the weight of his apron, two mortar shells in front and two behind, plus a rifle and bandoliers of ammunition. Crossing a creek he fell and filled the bag with water.

Entering Iba, eerie silence had greeted them, one of the strangest experiences they encountered. Not a soul awaited them. Then Filipinos who had fled to the mountains to escape imprisonment and who had valiantly held out through the long years of war came in from the hills just behind the soldiers, freed from their exile at last. The Japanese left the bridge at Iba ready to blow but a Filipino soldier sneaked in and pulled off the wires.

Jeff's appreciation for every branch of the military increased with each tale. The ground crews who had the dirty mop-up job deserved high respect, living in trenches, following the rough trails made by carabao-drawn [water buffalo] carts, fighting underbrush, prickly heat, and mud during the monsoon season, as well as the enemy. Unless they were fortunate enough to find a well with a pitcher pump installed by the

Americans who had dug them early in the occupation of the Philippines, they must push bamboo in a bank so water would come out. They would then drop halogen tablets in their canteens to purify the water, never drinking from a creek until it had been checked by the medics. If the person designated to bring food didn't reach them, it meant doing without. Sometimes they drank water from the water-cooled machine guns they carried.

Peril threatened the ships, from sky and sea alike. Earlier, a ship safely passed through a narrow entrance into a body of water with an island in the middle, located near New Guinea. It sailed around the buoy and swung back and forth on anchor with the tide, broadside to the inlet. According to scuttlebutt, when the crew went to breakfast they heard an explosion. A Japanese sub had thrown three torpedoes, one to each side and the third down the middle. The outside ones missed. The third, which should have hit the Allied ship dead center, hit the buoy!

Jeff's next mission would come soon and his body cried out for rest. Yet sleep evaded him and for the first time in months he allowed Candleshine to creep into his thoughts. Familiar anger that had hit like a Howitzer shell and done nearly as much damage to his emotions was offset by the image of her honest blue eyes. But time and the necessity of concentrating on his job had dulled his outrage. He remembered her sweetness, the trust and lack of pretense she had shown when his arms encircled her on the PT boat.

His jaw set. How ironic that if Candleshine had stayed a few more minutes she'd have learned marriage was out. He'd been ordered back to immediate duty and left with Dan Black a bare hour after the nurses and their patient headed for Australia.

He shifted his position, willed himself to sleep, and failed. Perhaps his talk with the major had triggered his rebellion. This ungodly mess had to end soon. When it did. . . .

A little smile curved his mobile lips and brightened his spirits. "Cedar Ridge, Washington," he murmured. "Go to sleep, Fairfax. The sooner this war ends, the sooner you can follow the gleam to Cedar Ridge." He smothered a laugh at his poetic flight, yawned, and fell into deep sleep.

Hours later he awakened to the now-familiar summons. Alert and determined, Jeff headed out for yet another mission. Sometimes it seemed he had never existed except here fighting, retreating, fighting again. Carson and the Laughing X might have existed in someone else's lifetime. It didn't seem possible that somewhere peace lay over the land. A wave of nostalgia for home and his horses, for Carson and the ranchhouse, and for distant mountains that stretched to the sky beyond the cedar-darkened foothills left him grinning. "Almost, I'd even be glad to see Lillian." He immediately shook his head. He must be getting dotty.

Without warning, the plane shuddered beneath his guiding hands. Bullets ripped into the cockpit. A quick glance showed him that American planes had already pounced like hawks on mice and dispersed the enemy fighters. Funny, his left leg felt numb. He glanced down. Wet patches showed he'd been hit.

The crazy antics of his plane warned of more trouble. "Hand me the first aid kit," Jeff told his copilot. He pressed the heel of his hand against his bleeding leg and applied pressure. "See if everyone else is okay."

"Copilot to crew. Everyone okay back there?"

"Yeah, but the plane ain't," came through the intercom. "We can't make it like this. We'll have to turn back."

"Just as well. Cap's hit." The copilot flicked off the intercom.

Jeff eased the plane in a wide arc. The numbness in his leg held but the initial shock wore off before they reached home base and he gritted his teeth in order to finish the course.

"Fire off a red flare," the copilot ordered when they arrived. "We're going to need an ambulance."

They landed. Jeff swung out on his right leg, dragged the left over, and crumpled. His brain felt fuzzy as it seemed a million devils were hammering into his leg. Finally he felt himself being lifted and carried into the twilight.

Jeff awakened to find the hatchet-faced major looming above him. The major grinned sourly. "If you wanted leave why didn't you just say so instead of going out and getting shot up?"

Jeff's gaze snapped to his heavily bandaged left leg. "Sir, how am I supposed to fly with that thing?" Disgust filled him.

"You won't be flying for some time. That leg of yours needs more attention than it can get here. So do you." The major's eyebrows met in a frown. "You bled bucketfuls and if it had been just a little farther coming back you wouldn't be here now. It's home for you and I pray to God we'll all be right on your heels getting there. There's a feeling in the air something climactic is about to happen. Don't ask me what, I don't know. I do know you've done more than your share."

"Thank you, sir. I'd rather stay. This little problem can't be that bad."

"You're under orders, Captain, and those orders are for you to be sent home." His wintry grin stilled Jeff's protests. "This time you have no choice."

After he'd gone Jeff stared at the doorway and felt like a slacker. What right had he to leave when needed? Grimly determined, he started to get out of bed and got the shock of a lifetime. The same crazy head-spinning he'd experienced after the accident left him as weak as the newborn calves he'd helped deliver back in Montana. Still ashamed but finally convinced, he sank back on the hard cot, glad for its support.

Dan Black came in once before Jeff left. "You're going by way of Australia?"

"Yeah, the scenic route," Jeff grumbled.

"Uh, mind doing me a favor, sir?"

"Can the sir. What do you want?"

Dan's steady eyes never left his captain's face. "Would you see if Jane's still at the hospital and if she is tell her nothing has changed?"

"That's all?" Jeff stared.

"She'll know what it means."

Understanding flowed through Jeff. *Nothing has changed.* If he and Dan were in opposite places with Candleshine in Australia, wouldn't his message be the same? He should never have pressured her. No wonder she seized the chance to get away and think! A rueful grin stretched his lips. War did strange things to people. If anyone had told him a few years earlier he'd fall in love, propose, and insist on marrying a girl he barely knew, he'd have laughed until his sides hurt.

"I'll tell her if she's there. When you get home, if you ever want an outdoor job — hard work and moderate pay — come to the Laughing X."

"I just may, if Jane likes Montana cattle ranches. We didn't have time to make real plans." Dan set his jaw. "I really don't know the things she loves. At first, I represented her brother. When I told her I cared and found out she did, too. . . ." His voice died.

"It's tough on everyone," Jeff quietly said, impressed with the truth in his radioman's simple statement, *We didn't have time.* God willing, there would be time, for them and thousands of other anxious couples.

An unexpected development hindered

Jeff's going home. In the Australian hospital his wounded leg acted up. Infection fought against medication and delayed the healing process. Concerned doctors dressed his leg daily and finally quelled his complaints. "All your fretting is hindering our efforts. If you want to keep that leg, start working with us instead of against us by wanting to get back in the middle of things. Granted, top pilots are needed but do you honestly think you're the only pilot in the U.S. Marines who can lick the Japanese?"

Jeff subsided, feeling the way he had when his second grade teacher stood him in the corner for fighting the class bully.

The minute he reached the hospital he had inquired about Jane. Not until he faithfully repeated Dan Black's message did he notice how pretty the nurse from No-Name Island had become. Or did the radiance in her eyes account for it?

She stopped in and visited when she could, but her busy schedule left little time.

Once he hesitated and asked, "Have you heard from Nurse Thatcher at all?"

"Twice, sir. She spent a lot of time in Cedar Ridge getting over the effects of the malaria and —"

"Malaria?"

"Yes, we kept her here for a time. Anyway,

the last letter came just a few months ago. She's back at Mercy Hospital in Seattle supervising the rehabilitation ward." After a moment she added, "And waiting with the rest of us for the war to end." Softness touched her eyes. "She asked about you, sir."

How ridiculous for his heart to drum against his ribs! "Oh?"

"She just wondered if I had ever seen or heard about you or Dan or Magee."

"Oh." Jeff felt let down in spite of the good news. Just his luck to have her fall in love with one of those on-the-spot men in her ward. The next minute he laughed and told Jane goodbye in case he got out before she had time to come again. Candleshine was not the type to jump from sweetheart to sweetheart. He'd known when he kissed her the very first time she embodied purity and untouched love. She also possessed valor and an overdeveloped sense of fair play. He bet she'd never let her heart get involved until she finished things up with a certain marine flyer. That thought alone made it easier to await his return to the States.

Jeff did not wait alone. The world also waited, for what they dared not conjecture. Every Allied victory, each setback sent waves around the globe. Stories leaked out confirming that the new developments in antimalarial therapy and drugs, the availability of blood derivatives, and the heroism and ingenuity of the medical corpsmen accounted for the saving of countless lives that other wars would have claimed. The world also watched as the upstart American vice-president assumed the reins of the presidency in April 1945. Could Harry S. Truman, even though he had worked with FDR until his death, succeed at the tremendous task he faced?

The answer came in early August. The U.S., Great Britain, and China warned Japan to surrender unconditionally or be destroyed. *Japan continued to fight.*

August sixth rocked the world.

An American B-29 bomber, the *Enola Gay*, carried and dropped the world's first atomic bomb to be used in war on Hiroshima. It destroyed five square miles and killed 80,000 to 100,000.

The world again waited.

Japan went on fighting.

On August ninth, the U.S. dropped a second atomic bomb, this time on Nagasaki, killing approximately 40,000.

Unable to withstand such wholescale destruction, Emperor Hirohito stepped into politics, despite the traditional hands-off policy of Japanese emperors. On August fourteenth Japan surrendered, but some of their leading military leaders committed suicide rather than accept the defeat of their dreams to control the world.

Japanese representatives and those from every Allied nation gathered on September second on the U.S.S. battleship *Missouri*, anchored in Tokyo Bay. When Japan signed the official surrender papers on what President Truman designated as V-J Day (Victory over Japan Day), World War II ended. Millions had died in a conflict based on greed and the desire for power.

American boys and men came home, old beyond their years. Some carried physical scars, but all brought emotional wounds with them. Candleshine doubled her efforts, then tripled them, demanding the best of herself and her staff. With the overseas fighting behind them, many still had long, painful fights ahead.

Yet in the quiet nights and busy days, hope never left her. Japanese internment camps were disgorging their long-held prisoners. Candleshine prayed Bruce and Winona would be among them, survivors of mistreatment and unspeakable conditions, but alive.

She also prayed for Connie. What kind of world would her friend face after imprisonment in her own country?

A hasty note from Jane bore the good news she'd be shipping out for America soon, and that *her husband* Dan Black would accompany her! They'd been married shortly after V-J Day.

We're seriously considering accepting Captain Jeffrey Fairfax's offer and settling on the Laughing X. Dan says after all the action he can never go back to a desk job. He wants to be free and whatever he wants will make me happy.

Captain Fairfax is already there. We finally licked the infection in his left leg and he won't lose it as we feared. As I mentioned when I wrote before, touch and go best described his situation. He seemed pleased that you had asked about him.

The letter fell from Candleshine's nerveless fingers. *Jeff hurt, so seriously they thought he'd lose a leg? Jane mentioned a letter. Why hadn't it come through?*

"Thank God he's all right," she whispered. A vision of Jeff as she last saw him danced in her mind. Tall, commanding, his eyes aglow with the prospect of their marriage. . . .

She clasped both hands around her knees. "Dear God, I failed him once," she cried in a broken voice. "More by not telling him of You than breaking my promise to become his wife. No matter how hard it is, when I see him again I will share my faith."

A few weeks later Candleshine received a summons on the ward to report to Miss Grey's office immediately. Her knees turned to pudding as she quietly gave orders to the nurse who substituted for her.

"Miss Grey may have new patients coming in," she scolded herself on the interminable walk down the halls and to the Supervisor of Nurses' office. Breathing deeply, she tapped.

"Come in," a male voice invited.

Candleshine stepped inside, stopped, then stared. With a glad cry she hurled herself at the tall, emaciated figure whose eyes glowed with light in an otherwise dead face.

Dr. Bruce Thatcher had come home.

Twelve

Candleshine clung to the beloved cousin she had feared dead in spite of her faith. An eternity later she voiced a remaining fear. "Winona?"

Bruce's deep voice did more to reassure her than anything else in the world. "Thin, nerves shattered, but alive and home."

Candleshine's head jerked up. "When can I see her?"

"Soon, but first let her family have her. She also needs rest. As soon as her parents agree, I'm taking her to Cedar Ridge to heal."

"As your wife?"

"How did you know?" Surprise punctuated each word.

"Sweeny stopped by a lifetime ago." Candleshine bit her quivering lips. "He told me what you said."

"Someday I intend to marry Winona but not until she can put the horror behind her."

Candleshine shivered at the somber look in his eyes. "Can you talk about it?"

His blue gaze returned to her. "I can, but I won't. Whatever you heard from Sweeny, plus any other accounts, is about a hundredth of what happened. The sooner those of us who survived forget it, the better." He grinned and a trace of the old Bruce surfaced. "Mind if we sit down? It's going to take a while to get enough decent food in me to get back my energy." He glanced around the office, longing in his face. "I can hardly wait to be back here working amid order, cleanliness, and supplies. Candleshine, one of the worst parts of the last years is feeling helpless to save people who should be alive now and who would have, given proper conditions."

She felt the anger behind his bitter tirade. "You're home, dear. As soon as you're ready, your work is waiting."

"I know." He stared directly into her face but Candleshine had the feeling his thoughts lay across the ocean in a distant land.

Sensing his awkward pause, he clumsily patted her shining short hair. "I guess Cedar Ridge is planning some kind of blow-out in honor of the boys coming home, including me, although I wasn't actually in the military. Can you come?"

"I wouldn't miss it." She smiled, a rainbow after rain. "If Winona feels like it, maybe she can come too."

"Don't push her in any way," Bruce warned. "So much happened in such a short time I'm not sure she ever had the time to deal with her fiancé's death at Pearl. If she wants to talk, let her. If she doesn't —" He lifted his shoulders expressively.

Candleshine walked out to the street with him. In a few hours he'd be in Cedar Ridge. She wished she were free of hospital duties and could go with him, but she knew his father and stepmother and Will and Trinity deserved time with him. Her heart ached at how gaunt his body had become. Yet as she took in the squared shoulders and the head held high, bared to the hazy autumn sun, she realized he was a man among men. A cousin to be proud of for all her life.

Remembering Bruce's admonition not to push, Candleshine took the precaution of calling the Allens before attempting to see them. Mrs. Allen said Winona was sleeping but she'd tell her when she awakened. Some of her fears as a mother spilled out. "She's terribly changed, of course. The worst thing is the dullness in her eyes. I think so often how they snapped with mischief and fun.

Candleshine, do you think my daughter will ever come back to me? To us?"

Candleshine's hand tightened on the telephone. "Yes, but she won't ever be the same person who went away." She took a deep breath. "Mrs. Allen, I didn't experience anything like what Winona lived through but it took me a long time to heal or even to talk about it."

"What should I do? How did your parents handle it for you?" Mrs. Allen asked anxiously.

A big lump formed in Candleshine's throat. "They simply loved me, didn't ask questions, and waited. They also prayed, a lot."

"Thank you so much." Candleshine could hear Winona's mother crying softly. "I'll tell her as soon as she's awake. Right now all she wants to do is sleep. The doctor says it's the best thing for her as she probably didn't get one single good night's rest the entire time she was held prisoner." She thanked Candleshine again and broke the connection.

Early that evening Winona returned the call. When Candleshine picked up the phone, the first words she heard were, "Little Sister?" Yet Winona's voice sounded flat and lifeless, unlike the vivacious, bubbling voice that could turn serious with concern over a younger nurse's problems.

Dear God, what shall I say? Candleshine silently prayed, but Winona spared her the need for small talk.

"When do you have time off? Not just an hour but an afternoon or day? Candleshine, I really want to see you."

The unspoken appeal released her tongue. "I'm scheduled for time off Friday but maybe I can get it changed." Surely Miss Grey would rearrange duties when she learned of Winona's need.

"Call me if you can."

"I will," Candleshine promised. She hesitated then added, "You must already know there's no one in the world I'd rather welcome as my new cousin when the time comes than you."

A little choking sound told her the ice jam around Winona had begun to crack. So did the quick "Bless you" before her friend hung up.

Miss Grey immediately rescheduled the nurses on the rehabilitation ward when Candleshine explained why she'd like time off earlier. "Tell Winona I expect her back here the minute she's ready, not one minute sooner or one minute later."

How true to form Miss Grey ran! Those

were the same words she had used when Candleshine approached her about returning to Mercy Hospital.

Although the few days at home hadn't overcome the telltale signs of imprisonment, Winona had regained a tiny bit of sparkle by the time Candleshine visited her. By silent mutual agreement they avoided talking about the war. Candleshine did tell how Sergeant Sweeny stopped by on his way home to recuperate. Winona laughed out loud at his calling Miss Grey a "grand old dame" and Candleshine caught the look of gratitude on Mrs. Allen's face.

"Sweeny made our stay on Corregidor a lot easier," Winona said before the familiar shadow fell back over her eyes.

"You and Bruce must have witnessed to him," Candleshine quickly said and was rewarded with a lifting of the shadow and a show of interest. She repeated the things Sweeny said and finished by saying, "I think Sweeny was well on his way to becoming a Christian, if not already there."

"I'm glad," Winona said softly. She reached a thin hand toward her friend and a poignant light made her finely drawn features beautiful. "A very few good things came out of being over there and my learning to rely on God for every minute of every day is number one." She added with a flash of the old Winona, "Bruce is number two!"

Candleshine just hugged her, too filled to speak. So all the prayers had born fruit. Yet hadn't she always known Bruce could never join his life with anyone who didn't believe and serve his God? A little tremor went through her. One by one things fell into place. First Bruce and Winona were home; soon Connie Imoto would return. Yet until Lieutenant, no, Captain Jeffrey Fairfax came back, the ragtag ends of the war would not be secured.

In the next few weeks Candleshine spent as much time as possible with Winona. Little by little, the thin, pale cheeks filled out. The dark shadows lurking in the black eyes slowly receded. Although quieter, in many ways Winona reverted back to the former beloved Big Sister with Candleshine except now the two nurses shared a more equal friendship due to experiences and passing years.

Connie Imoto came home before Thanksgiving. She called Candleshine immediately and arranged a meeting. Not in the lovely home that had been the Imotos' for years but in a small place they had found in a Seattle suburb. It would take years to get established again after their heavy losses due to relocation.

Candleshine almost dreaded the meeting but relief flooded her the moment she saw her tiny friend. Without being told, she knew Connie had kept her torch of faith in God and others burning.

Connie seemed reluctant to speak of the past except to share wonderful news. During the long weeks, months, and years of communal living, crowded into barracks, she had been able to minister both medically and spiritually. Her own refusal to harbor hate or resentment, and her firm belief that America would win the war and become the grand country that offered opportunity to all, influenced those about her.

"My parents have left the worship of the old gods," she rejoiced. "They accepted Christ just a few months ago. Candleshine, God's promise to bring good from evil came true in the camp, especially for the Imotos."

She sat quietly and lowered her voice to a whisper. "All of us agree, everything we lost, the freedom taken from us, is nothing compared with the priceless gift we now have. And God has spared my brother! He fought valiantly, earned the Purple Heart, and is nearly ready to work again."

"Are you coming back to Mercy?" Candleshine asked.

"Oh, yes. Miss Grey has an opening in pediatrics the first of January. That gives me time to get ready."

"Winona will be back, too, but I don't know when. Her family has agreed to lend her for a few weeks." Candleshine laughed. "Bruce is chomping at the bit waiting. He can't wait to show her Cedar Ridge in winter."

Sadness touched Connie's face. "I'd like to see her, if she's willing."

"Why wouldn't she be?" Honestly surprised, Candleshine blinked.

Connie glanced down at her interwoven fingers. "There are those who see me as the enemy."

Candleshine felt horror swim over her. "You don't mean you have had people treat you badly, after all you went through?"

Connie shook her shining dark head. "Not me, but friends have awakened to a cross burning in their yard and hooded figures chanting hate messages." The sadness spread and Connie raised her head. "For some, the war will not end. Ever."

Again Candleshine felt shame that people

could treat fellow Americans who had suffered and fought, bled and died, so outrageously.

She never forgot the meeting between Connie and Winona. The look that passed between the two shut her out. Although thousands of miles apart, her two friends had shared similar experiences. When their hands met in sincere friendship, Candleshine felt like crying. The symbolism of the mutual reaching out spoke volumes.

Winona left for Cedar Ridge. Candleshine made flying trips home when days off permitted the journey. The small town outdid itself welcoming back its war heroes. Thanksgiving 1945 mingled fervent blessings and mourning for those who no longer filled the empty chairs around family tables. Winona's stay in Cedar Ridge restored her health miraculously. She could go back to work in January and start planning for a June wedding.

In the midst of the excitement, and the idea that Bruce and all three women would again be serving at Mercy Hospital, Candleshine found herself restless. Jeff had been home for months in which she had expected a letter or a telephone call or visit. Instead, she heard nothing. She hesitated between wanting to take the initiative and letting things ride. What if she wrote and discovered he had found someone else?

That doesn't dismiss your promise to witness, her conscience reminded. Sometimes she considered asking for a leave of absence and simply showing up on his doorstep! He had asked her to visit, hadn't he? Would she be welcome? Or would a stern-faced man look at her as if she were a pesky tumbleweed blown in where it didn't belong?

"I'll hear at Christmas," she assured herself. "Then I can go from there." Deep inside she knew the real reason she could not contact Jeff lay in her relationship with her Heavenly Father. Her love for Jeff, born on a tropical island, had never died. At times dormant and hazy, now that she saw the trust and love between Bruce and Winona, her own feelings demanded recognition. She loved Jeff Fairfax and always would but first her allegiance belonged to God. As Christmas drew near, Candleshine inwardly fought the greatest battle of her life.

Two states away, Captain Jeffrey Fairfax struggled to become rancher Jeff Fairfax again. All of Carson's efforts hadn't kept the Laughing X up to prewar standards. The weathered foreman welcomed Jeff home with expressions of gratitude to God but abject apologies.

"I just couldn't get the right kind of help," he admitted as he beat dust from his faded Stetson. "Never hired an alien, though, just citizens and naturalized citizens or those who were workin' on becomin' Americans."

"So just where do we stand?" Jeff leaned back in his easy chair, stared at the fireplace, and shifted his left leg. Eager to ride and hike and see everything, now he paid for it. The jagged scars had healed but every doctor he'd consulted said he had to give the muscles time to strengthen after their forced inactivity from the infected shrapnel wounds.

"You may carry a slight limp," one doctor warned. His tired face relaxed into a grin. "A small price compared with the possible loss of your leg."

Yet Jeff sighed. Someday he planned to visit Cedar Ridge and a family named Thatcher. Would Candleshine welcome a lamed civilian when she'd fallen in love with a slightly-the-worse-for-wear but whole marine? He just bet she would, if she welcomed him at all. He scowled and Carson's dry comment roused him.

"No need to get black in the face like some thundercloud. We ain't that bad off."

He proceeded painstakingly to relate how he'd sold stock to the armed forces. "Prime steers," he announced proudly. "The buyers said they didn't get any better than ours."

"So what we have is smaller herds, fewer men, and no way to go but up?"

Carson cackled. "Beats me how a college feller like you can boil things down to practically nothin'. That's about it. Say, that new man of yours, Black, he's a tenderfoot but he sure is willin'." Carson snorted like a horse at a water trough. "I'll take one like him over a half-dozen know-it-alls like some that came and went while you were gone. I reckon they didn't like the workin' conditions."

Noticing Carson's smirk, Jeff mentally reckoned they didn't either. Anyone who didn't pull his weight on the Laughing X incurred Carson's legendary wrath. If a cowboy got a second chance and failed, Carson fed him his time and pointed him off the ranch.

"That little wife of Black's a mighty fine gal, too," Carson approved. "She up an' baked me an apple pie the other day that makes Cookie's stuff taste like sawdust."

"I'm glad they're working out," Jeff told him. "It's a long way from being a radioman to herding cattle."

"No longer than from being a pilot, I'd say." Carson swelled up like a pouter pigeon. "Jeff, are you goin' to be satisfied here on the ranch after all the fuss an' feathers an' excitement you saw?"

"I'll be content to spend the rest of my life right here in Montana." Jeff's quiet words spilled out more of what he'd gone through than anything he'd said since he got home. He amended the quick statement. "Sure, sometime I'll want to do some traveling when I can get away, but within the borders of the good old U.S. of A." He leaned forward, poked at the fire, and stared into the leaping flames.

"Know what, Carson? All the time I was overseas, I thought how I'd never really taken the time or trouble to get to know the country I was fighting for. Oh, I studied history and geography and all that stuff in school, but I want to go see Gettysburg and Washington, D.C., and Boston, all the places where our ancestors worked and fought so we could be free. It's a lot more important to me now that I know how high a price tag that freedom carries."

"Anytime you want to go, it's fine with me," Carson approved. "I kept the place goin' through a war. Seems like I should be able to keep it goin' while you gallivant around the country." His twinkling eyes showed he understood.

A little pool of silence fell and Jeff stretched. Hard to believe that just months before he lay in an Australian hospital wondering if he'd lose a leg. God had been good.

Carson cleared his throat. His bright eyes peered out from beneath his thatch of white hair. "Say, Jeff, that Grover woman showed up once after you left."

"What?" Jeff grimaced when his sudden movement sent a thrust of pain through his leg. "I thought you'd tied a can to her when you told her I'd never be anything than a rancher."

"Me too, but she up and said she'd been thinkin' things over. This was after the papers got hold of your dunk into the ocean an' wrote up how our local hee-ro saved his radioman."

Jeff waved it aside. He hated being called a hero for doing what any decent man would do in the same circumstances. "So?"

"So I gently but firmly reminded her nothin' had changed an' you couldn't wait to get home and start punchin' cows again." Carson's grin failed to hide his satisfaction. "She sorta sighed like she wished things were different but she didn't come back. A little later I read in the paper about the marriage of Miss Lillian Grover to Major Some-body or Other."

"Glad to hear it." Jeff grinned back. "How come some women try and put their brand on a guy when he isn't willing?"

"Human nature, I guess." Carson stood and straightened to full height. His persuasive voice sent color to Jeff's hair. "How come you didn't find yourself a girl as nice as Jane while you were gone? Or was she the only one around and Black beat you to it?" His keen eyes narrowed. "Or maybe you did?"

Jeff dropped his head to keep from blurting out that he had found someone far above the practical, devoted Jane. If he told Carson, would his old foreman understand? Had Jane said anything that had made Carson suspicious?

While he hesitated, his foreman's work-worn hand fell on his shoulder. "Boy, once we agreed you have to pick someone like her." He nodded toward the treasured picture of Jeff's parents. "When you do, fetch her home. Don't let anythin' stop you." He tightened his hold then quietly walked out, leaving Jeff to watch the dying embers in the fireplace. If he could "fetch" Candleshine to the Laughing X, he'd never let her go.

Thirteen

Sadness pervaded Mercy Hospital when Bruce received word that Sweeny had been killed in action. Candleshine grieved on her own account, remembering the cheerful sergeant who brought her word of Bruce and Winona. Yet she rejoiced that they had been able to witness to Sweeny and felt sure from what he'd said to her the brusque soldier knew the Lord.

A subdued but ecstatic Sally Monroe came home and asked Candleshine to be her bridesmaid in the spring. Her Jim had come through unscathed. Sally's face glowed. "We're sure now, but it's been so long we want to get reacquainted.

"Besides," she added practically. "With the rest of our lives to be married there's no hurry."

Candleshine stifled a sigh. Jim and Sally. Bruce and Winona. Even Connie Imoto shyly confessed interest in a friend her brother met in the service. Sometimes Candleshine felt excluded from the small circles of love within her big circle of family and friends. *Did Jeff ever think of her,* she wondered wistfully. *If so, had time cushioned the shock and left pleasant memories?* Many times each day she lifted her gaze from her work and thought of his lean face, his laughing eyes that held tenderness, and his white smile and bronzed face.

Four days before Christmas, Miss Grey again summoned Candleshine from her ward work. Breathless, the student nurse who came for her just missed breaking the hospital and training school rule of no running except in a dire emergency. "Miss Grey wants you *now*," she blurted out.

In spite of the dozens of times she'd been called to Miss Grey's office, Candleshine's heart never failed to skip a beat. Today proved no exception. As usual, she took deep breaths and slowly released them.

"A long distance call came for you and I asked them to call back in ten minutes," Miss Grey said. Her eyes looked apprehensive, something Candleshine had never seen before. "The operator said it was an emergency."

The phone on her desk shrilled and she snatched it. "Yes? She's here. Just a moment, please." She put her hand over the receiver. "Shall I stay?"

"Please." Candleshine reached for the phone. "Candace Thatcher speaking."

"Candleshine, it's Jane, Jane Black."

Candleshine gripped the phone more tightly. "Yes, Jane, what's wrong?" She clearly heard the intake of breath before Jane faltered.

"Jeff Fairfax is badly hurt. He's delirious and calling for you. Can you come?"

The universe spun but Miss Grey's discipline held, although Candleshine felt the blood drain from her face. "What happened?"

"He thought his leg had healed but it evidently hadn't. He and Dan rode out this morning to check on the stock. Jeff's horse stumbled in a gopher hole. He tried to kick free of the stirrup but his bad leg got caught. He was thrown and dragged."

"I'll be there as soon as I can," Candleshine promised.

"Dan will meet you in Missoula. That's where they took Jeff." Jane's voice broke. "Candleshine, please hurry."

"I will." She cradled the phone and whirled toward Miss Grey. "I have to leave for Montana immediately. The officer I met while in the Pacific, he's hurt again. He needs me now." A little glow softened some of the ice inside her. Once, no, twice, she had failed Jeff. *She would not fail him this time.*

"Go pack what you need for an indefinite stay," Miss Grey ordered. "I'll check on transportation." By the time Candleshine reached the door, the Superintendent of Nurses had dialed. She looked up while waiting for her number to ring. "I'll page Dr. Thatcher and you can see him before you go."

Candleshine boarded a small, chartered plane arranged for by Miss Grey and Bruce when they discovered no commercial airline flew east for several hours. Bruce wisely asked for no explanations, but hugged his cousin, who looked up at him with intense blue hurting eyes. "We'll be praying."

Comforted, she climbed into the charter plane and watched the pilot's skillful hands maneuver the controls.

Jane met her at the Missoula landing field. Every freckle stood out and the strain she couldn't hide made Candleshine's heart plummet. "He's about the same," Jane answered her friend's unspoken demand. "His body took terrible punishment before Dan could stop the horse and free Jeff."

"Just how bad is it?" She had to know.

"He almost wrecked his left leg and the doctors suspect his skull is fractured."

Candleshine bit her lower lip until she tasted blood. "What are his chances?"

Jane hesitated, her eyes troubled.

"Jane, *what are his chances?*"

"Not good," the other nurse whispered. "I overheard two doctors discussing him and they're not sure he can stand surgery but without it —" Her silence finished the sentence.

From deep within came strength and peace. Candleshine drew herself up to her full height. Her eyes blazed. "Jeffrey Fairfax is going to lick what odds the doctors give him. He's going to get well. He can't die. I won't let him and I don't believe God will either."

"Then tell him so," Jane whispered. She guided her friend out into the beginning of an old-fashioned Montana blizzard, drove the ranch Jeep to the hospital, and waited while Candleshine hurriedly changed to one of the uniforms she brought with her. "It's all arranged that you'll special him," she said. "They're always shorthanded, like any hospital. I've even come in from the Laughing X and helped out a few times." She glanced outside and looked worried. "Good thing you got here when you did. No small plane could make it through what Carson says is ahead."

"Carson?" She tried to remember what Jeff had said about him.

"The ranch foreman and a Godsend." Jane's lips quivered. "He has the same faith you do and refuses to believe anything but that 'the boy,' as he calls Jeff, will heal." She led Candleshine down the hall. Outside a private room a weather-beaten, white-haired man with the keenest eyes Candleshine had ever faced stopped pacing and shook the nurse's hand. Without a word, Candleshine knew Carson could be depended on in what lay ahead. She gratefully clung to his hand, instantly bonding with the man Jeff loved next to his own father.

"Nurse Thatcher?" A kind-faced woman several years older than the two women beckoned from the open door. She made no effort to whisper but kept a normal voice that stilled the hard beating of Candleshine's heart. "Captain Fairfax — we still think of him like that — has been asking for you. We don't know how much he can hear at the moment but I know he'll be glad you've come."

Candleshine stepped close to the hospital bed, welcoming yet dreading the moment. She gasped. How little Jeff had changed from the time she cared for him in No-Name Hospital! A little white in the dark hair escaped the bandages near his temples but otherwise he looked the same. A few new lines had been graven in his haggard face that hadn't been there when they laughed and fell in love.

"Go ahead and speak to him," the older nurse said. She slipped back out into the hall and Candleshine heard her talking with Jane and Carson.

"Jeff?" She knelt by his bed and cradled his limp hand in hers. "It's Candleshine. I'm here."

Over and over she repeated the words. Sometimes she thought they penetrated the dim recesses of his unconsciousness. At other times she wondered if he'd ever be alert enough to hear her. A strange time began for her, one that demanded her finest skills. Spelled by Jane so the regular nurses could care for the increased patient load from the blizzard, the hospital room and the small room nearby where she and Jane rested became her whole world. A thousand prayers rose and fell when Jeff sank so low the doctors scheduled surgery in spite of his weakened condition. A simple, "Thy will be done," became the hardest prayer Candleshine had ever offered.

Because of her emotional involvement, the surgeon absolutely refused to allow Candleshine to assist. Never had hours dragged as did those in which the surgeon "patched Jeff's head," as Carson said. Yet the presence of the foreman who for once in his life had turned over the handling of the Laughing X to his cowboys and who stayed at the hospital day and night meant comfort for Candleshine.

"The way I figure it," he told her when for the dozenth time she paced the waiting room floor, "it's like this. If the good Lord's wantin' Jeff for some special work up there with Him, why, He knows Jeff will be willin'. If not —"

Candleshine's soul snatched the words. "Jeff will be willing? You mean he's a *Christian?*"

Carson's eyes rounded. "Of course. His daddy an' mother taught him from the Bible from the time he could sit a pony. When they died in the train accident, Jeff went through a spell of doubtin', which is natural like." Carson's eyes took on a faraway look. "I don't see that God holds that against us." He smiled and wiped years from his face. "Anyway, since he got back from overseas there's been a big change in him."

Candleshine stiffened.

"He's quieter, but when he talks it shows without him sayin' that somehow, somewhere out there in the Pacific the boy made his peace with his Master an' those doubts disappeared. Would you be knowin' about that? Jane mentioned, real casual like, you were on that tropical island with them."

All this time I've wondered and worried for nothing. Candleshine felt dazed. *Why, Jeff must have taken for granted from things he let drop that I knew he loved the Lord. What have I done?*

Candleshine helplessly sank to a chair and hitched it closer to Carson's. "If you don't mind, I want to tell you a story. . . ." She faltered.

"Does it have a happy ending?" the old foreman asked quietly.

She twisted her fingers in her lap. "I — I don't know." She fumbled for words and at last told him everything from the time Jeff arrived on No-Name Island carrying his badly wounded radioman and friend Dan Black. If Jane had shared some or all of what she knew, Carson didn't betray it with even a blink. He just listened and when Candleshine finished, he patted her hand. "Don't you s'pose God knows all about it, girl? You couldn't help bein' sent to Australia any more than Jeff could help leavin' Guadal-canal just after you went."

For the first time she pieced together what happened that critical day so long ago. In a few well-chosen words Carson made her see what she'd been unable to comprehend on her own.

"I still don't understand," she whispered. "When he got home, after all this time, he must have known I wanted to see him."

Carson's eyebrows drew together in a straight line. "The boy's proud. As long as he limped so much, do you think he'd come knockin' at your door? Not Captain Jeffrey Fairfax. He'd want to march up as straight an' tall as he was after you nursed him back to health out there in the Pacific theater." Carson scowled. "Now that he's busted up that leg even more, it may take some convincin' before he sees it doesn't matter."

"How could it?" Candleshine cried. "The only thing that ever held me back was feeling I'd promised to marry a man I barely knew and who might not be a Christian. As if a limp mattered!"

"Tell the boy that, when he's better." Carson grabbed a handkerchief from his pocket and blew his nose loudly. "Best medicine he could get."

"I will." But Candleshine silently added, *if*

I get the chance. At least part of her prayer had been answered. Even if Jeff never regained consciousness, never knew she had come to him, he belonged to the Lord, now and forever. She bowed her head and gave thanks.

An exultant voice cut into her mind. "Well, that boy of yours is one tough nut, Carson." The beaming surgeon strode toward them. "Came through fine and unless complications arise he's going to make it." The next moment the speechless surgeon found himself encircled in the arms of a laughing, crying nurse. "Why, Nurse Thatcher!" Yet he couldn't help grinning when she mumbled, "Thank you!" and fled.

The hours after the surgery passed almost as slowly as those before and during it. To Candleshine's disappointment, Jeff's doctors ordered her to call Jane and turn her patient over to her the moment he stirred.

"I understand it's been some time since he saw you," one explained. "Even joy can bring shock and that's the last thing he needs at this stage." He must have noticed her drooping shoulders and down-turned mouth. "You want what's best for him, don't you?"

"Of course." She put away her feelings and lifted her chin.

"It shouldn't be for long. In the meanwhile, why don't you go see the Laughing X? The storm's let up and Carson says he has to go check on Black and the others." His grin showed he knew and understood Carson perfectly.

"Why, maybe I will, since I'm about to be fired from my job," she said smiling.

"Any time you want a job here, it's yours," the doctor retorted. "Any chance you might be moving to Montana in the near future?"

She felt soft color steal up from her uniform collar. "I might."

"I thought so." He grunted. "Remember, you've got a job when you want it."

Candleshine had never thought she'd find a place so lovely in winter as Cedar Ridge. Yet the Laughing X, sleeping under its white blanket, did strange things to her. She ignored Carson's dry comment when they reached the ranchhouse that her first trip across the threshold should have been as a bride and reveled in the homey, warm atmosphere. The photograph of Jeff's parents drew her like a magnet. "It's like coming home," she murmured.

Carson crossed his arms and looked pleased. "Say, instead of lettin' Jeff know you're here, why don't you just stay with us until he comes home?"

Candleshine whipped around. "You mean be here in his own home when he arrives? I wouldn't dare!"

"Why not? Jane will be back in a few days an' until then you'll have the house to yourself. I have my own place."

Her eyes darkened. "But what if he doesn't want me?"

Carson didn't move a muscle. "He will."

Her eyes sparkled. "All right, I'll stay, but it's on your head if Jeff throws me out when he gets here!"

For a week, Candleshine stayed on the Laughing X. She had long ago written her parents the story of her romance and Christmas had flown by during the time of extreme concern over Jeff. January began and she knew both Winona and Connie were back nursing at Mercy Hospital. A little pang filled her. If she and Jeff married, when would she see them again? Or Cedar Ridge? Yet western Montana and western Washington weren't really so far apart. The Scripture about leaving others and cleaving together came to her. With Jeff she could be happy anywhere. And to think she'd spent weeks, months, and even years miserable and waiting!

On a brilliant late January day, Jeff came home, after pestering his doctors for more than a week. "Look, I'm too hard-headed to let a fall keep me down," he told them. "So what if my leg's going to be in a cast for awhile? Carson can play nursemaid, can't he?" He scowled at the cast then relaxed. "At least it will be gone by spring." He stretched. "Can't wait to get back outdoors."

"You're hopeless," his doctor told him.

"Yeah," Jeff agreed amiably. "How about it?"

"Well, since you'll have a nurse right there on the ranch I guess it will be all right." The doctor fixed a stern gaze on his unwilling patient. "You've got to promise me you'll do exactly what she says."

"Sure. Jane knows her stuff."

"Jane?" The doctor coughed. "Oh yes, Nurse Black. Funny how I'm never good at names." He laughed his way out of the room, to Jeff's astonishment.

Left alone, he wrinkled his forehead and tried to remember. Fever and delirium did odd things to a person. He'd have sworn he heard Candleshine speaking to him when he was down and almost out. He shook his head and looked at the blue and white day outside the window. Just when he'd been almost over that limp he had to pull the fool stunt of falling off a horse. A wry grin tilted his lips. "Man comes through a world war and gets hurt worse right in his own backyard!" How long would it take to stand straight?

"Lord, am I wrong? Is it pride that's keeping me from contacting her?" he prayed. "Thank You for bringing me through all this and help me do Your will."

He felt better but the wheels of his mind began to turn in giant circles. By the next day he admitted that until he saw or heard from Candleshine he'd never get his life completely back to normal. That afternoon he begged paper and pen from a nurse and wrote a letter to Cedar Ridge, Washington. *We have some unfinished business,* he began.

Jeff wrote until his hand cramped. He poured out all his anger, then the growing realization of how much he asked from Candleshine. *Too much, too soon.* The words haunted him even after he licked the envelope.

Carson showed up a few minutes later and Jeff thrust the letter at him before he changed his mind. "Mind mailing this for me?"

Carson glanced at the address.

"Hey, old-timer, you look like you just saw a ghost."

Keen eyes bored into the patient. "Maybe I did, boy." Carson chuckled, obviously over whatever ailed him for a moment. "Yes, sir, I'll see this gets delivered right an' proper!" He only stayed a little while and went out, still chuckling.

"What's so funny about this place, anyway?" Jeff demanded of the empty room. "Or is it me?" He twitched and paid for it. "Ouch! If people around here were in my position they wouldn't find things so all-fired funny!"

The next day the doctor released him. Jeff felt better than he had since he returned from overseas. At least he had taken the first step toward straightening things out with Candleshine. If she had found someone else, or if she couldn't care for a man with a bad leg, so be it. If not — Jeff felt his heart pound. How she'd love the Laughing X as he now saw it! Even her beloved Cedar Ridge couldn't beat this scenery. One of these days he'd find out for himself. This cast wouldn't be around forever. By spring, depending on how she answered, he'd be in fit condition to take a little trip to Cedar Ridge and Seattle to see a certain nurse with short, fluffy fair hair and wildflower-blue eyes.

Suddenly aware of the way Carson fidgeted when they got to the ranch, Jeff demanded, "What's wrong with you?"

"Uh, I was just wonderin' if it's better to prepare a person for a surprise or just to let it happen."

"Surprise!" Jeff glared. "Don't tell me the boys are up to some big welcome home something. You know I hate a fuss."

"I wouldn't exactly say the boys are up to somethin'." But Carson's chuckle did little to soothe Jeff. It would be just like him to arrange a party when all Jeff wanted was to rest. He carefully hoisted himself out of the Jeep, leaned a little on Carson, and hopped to the house, favoring the leg in the cast. By the time he got inside and settled on the couch in front of the fire he'd had it. "Carson, how about a cup of coffee?"

A slight rustle and a light fragrance warned him. *Surely Lillian hadn't barged in again. Married or not, it would be just like her! Probably Jane had come to make sure he followed doctors' orders.*

He glanced around, stared, and rubbed his eyes and stared again. Had his fever returned? *"You? Here?"*

"For always if you want me." Candleshine ran to the couch, her eyes glowing in the firelight. "Jeff, can you forgive me?" All the time of bittersweet memories crashed in on her. "I didn't know you were a Christian. I couldn't face marrying someone I'd only known a short time and —"

"But my letter," he said hoarsely. "I just wrote yesterday. How did you get here so fast?"

She drew the letter from her uniform pocket. "I've been here since the day you got hurt."

"Then it *was* you! You stayed with me and talked to me. Candleshine, beloved, you'll never leave me again, will you? Once I asked too much." He pulled back from her reaching arms, caught her by the shoulders, and looked deep into her eyes. "I'll always limp. Does it matter?"

Not a flicker of doubt shadowed her clear eyes. "I'd love you if you had no legs, Jeff."

Warm drops on his hands convinced him more than words.

"You'll be my wife as soon as I get better?"

A flood of color rushed through her fair skin. "I'm going to be your wife as soon as my family can come," she told him. "We can't very well ask Jane to stay with us and play chaperone while you mend, can we?"

Jeff's inarticulate cry answered her question. The same strong arms that had protected her on the PT boat reached and gathered her close. In the tawny firelight

Candleshine saw the love in Jeff's eyes that matched her own.

The war at last was over and Candleshine's torch burned bright and clear.

About the Author

Colleen L. Reece is a prolific author with over sixty published books. With the popular *Storm Clouds over Chantel,* Reece established herself as a doyenne of Christian romance.